Destined for Me

Also From Corinne Michaels

The Salvation Series
Beloved
Beholden
Consolation
Conviction
Defenseless
Evermore – 1001 Dark Nights Novella
Indefinite
Infinite

The Hennington Brothers Series
Say You'll Stay
Say You Want Me
Say I'm Yours
Say You Won't Let Go: A Return to Me/Masters and Mercenaries
Novella

Second Time Around Series
We Own Tonight
One Last Time
Not Until You
If I Only Knew

The Arrowood Brothers Series
Come Back from Me
Fight for Me
The One for Me
Stay for Me
Destined for Me

Willow Creek Valley Series
Return to Us
Could Have Been Us
A Moment for Us
A Chance for Us

Rose Canyon Series
Help Me Remember

Destined for Me

A Come Back for Me/Say You'll
Stay Crossover Novella

By Corinne Michaels

1001 DARK NIGHTS
PRESS

Destined for Me
A Come Back for Me/Say You'll Stay Crossover Novella
By Corinne Michaels

1001 Dark Nights

Copyright 2023 Corinne Michaels
ISBN: 979-8-88542-027-3

Foreword: Copyright 2014 M. J. Rose

Published by 1001 Dark Nights Press, an imprint of Evil Eye Concepts, Incorporated

Dedication

This is for all the professionals who do the jobs I write about, and still continue to love me after I'm sure I screw it up!

One Thousand and One Dark Nights

Once upon a time, in the future…

*I was a student fascinated with stories and learning.
I studied philosophy, poetry, history, the occult, and
the art and science of love and magic. I had a vast
library at my father's home and collected thousands
of volumes of fantastic tales.*

*I learned all about ancient races and bygone
times. About myths and legends and dreams of all
people through the millennium. And the more I read
the stronger my imagination grew until I discovered
that I was able to travel into the stories... to actually
become part of them.*

*I wish I could say that I listened to my teacher
and respected my gift, as I ought to have. If I had, I
would not be telling you this tale now.
But I was foolhardy and confused, showing off
with bravery.*

*One afternoon, curious about the myth of the
Arabian Nights, I traveled back to ancient Persia to
see for myself if it was true that every day Shahryar
(Persian: شهریار, "king") married a new virgin, and then
sent yesterday's wife to be beheaded. It was written
and I had read that by the time he met Scheherazade,
the vizier's daughter, he'd killed one thousand
women.*

Something went wrong with my efforts. I arrived in the midst of the story and somehow exchanged places with Scheherazade – a phenomena that had never occurred before and that still to this day, I cannot explain.

Now I am trapped in that ancient past. I have taken on Scheherazade's life and the only way I can protect myself and stay alive is to do what she did to protect herself and stay alive.

Every night the King calls for me and listens as I spin tales. And when the evening ends and dawn breaks, I stop at a point that leaves him breathless and yearning for more. And so the King spares my life for one more day, so that he might hear the rest of my dark tale.

As soon as I finish a story... I begin a new one... like the one that you, dear reader, have before you now.

Chapter One

HADLEY

"It's too bad my client had to walk away from your attempt at fixing the contract," a deep voice that has taunted me for five years says from the edge of my office door.

Cayden. Fucking. Benson-Hennington.

The bane of my existence. It doesn't matter that I am an associate at my law firm. That I have more billable hours than any other associates—and probably more than him—even though he was hired at the firm we both interned at while I was not. I swear, it's his life's mission to always be one step above me.

Not today, Satan.

"Well, your client is an idiot, and should take the deal I presented. Believe me, you won't get a better chance to fix the mess you made. There won't be another offer."

His wide grin makes my stomach flip. "We'll see."

"Yes, I think we will. Was there something you needed?" He steps inside—uninvited I might add—and takes a seat. "By all means, make yourself comfortable."

"Look, Hadley, we both know that your client was asking for way too many concessions. To have two seats on the board would give them controlling votes. Come on, you know that was an error."

"Maybe so, but it wasn't my error, it was yours."

To be fair, it wasn't really his error. Cayden took over this negotiation after his client used another firm who clearly botched the contract. Still, it's his issue at the very least.

"No, but it is my mess and I plan to clean it up. By the end of this, my beautiful nightmare, you will be walking out with less than you came in with."

He's so arrogant, ugh, I want to kiss him. I mean punch him. Punch. Not kiss. No, no, been there and done that. Never again.

"So you want to rob these people of their entire life's work?"

"I want my client to get what they deserve."

I bet he does. This man has no soul. "Do you forget where you come from?" I ask.

Cayden grew up in Tennessee. His family owns a horse ranch that they have had for generations. Literally a blue collar, farming family.

The same as my clients. They were approached to sell their land, giving up their legacy, all so his client's company can dismantle it and make it into a resort or a strip mall.

Therefore, I don't think asking for something to help safeguard either of those from happening is a concession they shouldn't ask for. It's only fair that their children have at least a little left at the end of this.

"Of course, I know where I came from."

"And if this were your parents, how would you advise them?"

He leans forward, resting his forearms on his knees. His green eyes fixed on me. "That's where we differ, Arrowood…these aren't my parents. They're my clients and my goal is to get them everything they want."

I get up and walk around the desk, resting my ass just on the edge. His gaze moves down to my legs and up, lingering a bit on my chest. I watch as a flicker of desire flashes across his face, and I wonder if he's picturing me naked. Remembering that stupid night we spent together in college.

Lord knows I am—not. Nope, I'm not. I won't. Because it was a mistake. Sure, I'll go with that.

Good thing I have an incredible poker face.

"What are you thinking about?" his voice is low and husky.

You and me on the floor, ripping each other's clothes off. Or the desk, that would be equally fine.

"I'm thinking about how arrogant and ridiculous you are. You came to my office to what?" I keep my tone even.

"To talk some sense into you and tell you to have your clients stop this bullshit and take the revision. It's a good amount of money and it's fair."

I roll my eyes and huff. "My clients are not going to do that because, as you said, my goal is to protect them and their legacy. And the original deal has two seats on the boar, where your *revision*, has none."

Cayden grabs his suit jacket he had draped over his legs, rises, and tosses it over his shoulder. "Well, tell them the deal is off and we'll be buying the property once it's in foreclosure—without *any* seats on the board."

I shrug. "I will. Good luck to your client for not taking their incredibly generous counter and good luck finding another piece of land. We have other options, Cayden."

The both of us are losing here, but there's not a chance in hell I will let him know that. I don't actually have another solution.

My clients need to sell. They're in an incredible amount of debt and this was a great chance to sell the back part of their property and merge two companies into being a more symbiotic resort. At least that was what was promised. Then, in the last two weeks, the talks of that changed. They were discussing building ordinances and codes for something much larger than just a small resort.

He takes two steps toward me, leaning in so I can smell his cologne and feel his heat.

God, he smells so freaking good. It's musky with an edge of something warm at the end that tickles my nose.

And then there's his body. Oh how I wish I didn't remember it in perfect detail. How his muscles flexed beneath my touch or the way his voice sounded as he sighed my name.

However, right now, we're not having sex. We're having a legal war.

"I've missed this," the rasp in his voice is like a caress. "It's not fun when we don't get to battle each other."

Yeah, it's like freaking foreplay only I end up orgasm-less.

"Do you know what I miss?" I ask, playing his game.

"What, beautiful?"

I press my hand against his chest, standing and pushing him toward my office door. He grins and it's the cat ate the canary kind, where he thinks he's winning whatever game we're playing.

When his back hits the wall, I run my hand down his chest, looking up at him through my lashes. "I miss…" I wait, letting the tension build. And it's definitely rising. "The way…" I open my office door, and step back. "You look when you're leaving. Goodbye, Cayden. Have a swell day and I'll be going over the preliminary offer to see where I can counter for damages if it falls apart."

He releases a laugh and shakes his head. "I'll see you soon. Count on it."

When he walks out, I close the door behind him, and rest my head on the solid oak panel. "Yeah, that's what I'm afraid of."

Chapter Two

CAYDEN

"I think you should reevaluate," I tell my client over the phone. When I got back to my office, I read every word of the contract my predecessor wrote. I knew it had issues. It was sloppy and absolutely not how I would've done it, but it was what it was and I figured this would go smoothly when I agreed to take over.

As soon as I saw it was Hadley Arrowood as opposing counsel on the acquisition, I immediately realized we were screwed.

There are not many lawyers I've faced who are as smart and cunning when it comes to these types of cases. Her eye for detail tells me she already found the issues and it's why she's playing hardball.

"And what would you have us do? Put the two failing business owners on the board who can shut down what we want?"

I lean back in my chair, pinching the bridge of my nose. "Legally, I'm advising you to do that or you're going to have to pay what you offered, their legal fees, as well as damages."

"No," my client, Mike, says. "We offered them a fair deal."

"Yes, and you also have issues with the contract you signed."

"What other options do we have?"

I look out the window of my Manhattan office, watching the traffic below. "Let me think on it and I'll call you back." There's a solution out there, I just need some time to think it through.

"Thanks, Cayden."

"No problem, Mike. Give me a day or two and let me see what I come up with."

"Sounds good."

I start to pace because I think better on my feet, but each solution I debate, I remember who's on the other side of the case. Hadley is very good at her job. When I'm opposing her, I have to be at my best.

"Cayden?" my assistant, Debra, calls through the intercom.

"Yes?"

"Mr. Tobias would like to see you."

Great. Just what I need…

Don't get me wrong, Paul Tobias is a great guy to work for. He's easy going, and doesn't micromanage—as long as you're bringing in clients, billable hours, and results.

Today, I didn't close the deal, which I promised I would have.

I head down the hall, straightening my tie before his secretary, Rachel, nods me through.

"Hennington, how goes it?" Paul asks as I enter.

"Good, how about yourself?"

He smiles, closing the folder he was reviewing. "Can't complain. How did today's negotiations go? I'm ready to have another one in the books."

I take a seat and prepare myself for a possible ass-chewing. "It's not done yet, but we'll get there."

"Not done, why?"

"The previous firm he used to draw up the tentative contract did a piss poor job. I'm working on getting things amended to better protect our clients. Opposing counsel is…difficult."

Paul opens the file again, scanning the page. "Hadley Arrowood?"

"That's the one."

"You should be a pro at handling her by now."

Does anyone really handle her? I don't think so. She's smart, strategic, and sexy as hell. Not that the last part has anything to do with her as a lawyer, it's just the truth.

"Well, sir, I am already dealing with one strike against me. The contract is garbage and Hadley knows it. She's not going to back down, and honestly, if it were me, I wouldn't either."

"Are you saying you can't deal with the case?" he counters.

"No. I'm saying it's going to take me a little bit of time and creative thinking to get around it."

His mouth sets into a thin line. "Okay, I had another case I was hoping to add you to, but I want this wrapped up first."

"Which case?" I ask, because if it's the new merger I consulted on, I want it. I worked my ass off to get them in the door and I'm not about to let it go to Bob, who hasn't brought anyone here in years, but is still making the most money while doing the least work.

"The publishing houses."

Fuck. I knew it. "Paul, with all due respect, that case was mine. They weren't even sure they should merge and I was the one who convinced them it was time."

Paul shrugs one shoulder. "That may be, but you're tied up and I am not going to give them time to change their mind. If you're able to get the other case cleaned up, then this one is yours."

I get to my feet, a fire in my veins that wasn't there before. "I'll get it done and then I want my client."

Paul stands as well. "Then I suggest you get to it and remind me why hiring you and not Hadley Arrowood was the right move."

I plan to do exactly that.

Chapter Three

HADLEY

I have two voicemails from Cayden. The first was an hour ago, asking about setting up another meeting where we could discuss any options that weren't on the table before. The second one, which came in four minutes after the first, informs me he'll be at my office soon to discuss what we didn't discuss from the first call.

I ring down to the front desk and tell them not to let him up. I am not about to be railroaded by him, which is his tactic.

Since he's so eager, which he didn't seem to be earlier, I'll let him sweat it out. I check my cellphone, and have a text from my mom and one from my roommate, Melanie, who happens to be my cousin.

Mom: Hi honey, I hope you're doing well. I know it's a little early, but I am planning to have Christmas at our house this year and really want you to come home. Your father and I miss you!

I smile at that. My mother is so cute. I missed last year because of work, this time I will do everything in my power to be there.

Me: A little early? It's the first week of June!
Mom: Yes, I know, but I am giving you six month's notice so you have no excuses!
Me: Okay… I can't wait to see you and I miss you and Dad.
Mom: We're not that far from the city.

She's right, but going home is a hassle and the last two times my train was delayed four hours. Which meant I had practically no time before I had to head back here.

Me: Maybe I can come home for Fourth of July.
Mom: That would make us so happy. Side note: Uncle Declan is going to be in the city this weekend so don't be surprised if you get a visit.
Me: Thanks for the heads up!

I love my uncles, but they drive Melanie and I crazy with their check-in visits they claim are coincidences. Uncle Declan didn't start coming into the city frequently until we moved here and my father convinced him to have an office close by.

Mom: Of course. I know he's a pain in the you know what.

Me: Yes, but we love him anyway. I have to run. Love you!

Mom: Love you more.

Then I check Melanie's text.

Melanie: Pizza or Thai?

That's a no-brainer.

Me: Pizza! Uncle Dec is in town, keep the lights off and don't answer the door. Also, I hate Cayden. Just in case you thought that may have changed. It hasn't.

Melanie: My mom sent me a warning text too. As for the Cayden part, can't wait to hear this.

I bet she can't. Poor Mel had to listen to my emotional breakdown after we slept together. I was so stupid that night. Of all the people I decided to hook up with, it was him. I'll never make that mistake again.

After tossing my phone in my bag, I shut my computer down, grab my laptop, pop my earbuds in, and head home. Our apartment is an adorable rent controlled two bedroom in SoHo. It's tiny, but neither of us care considering the location in Manhattan—and the price.

"Mel?" I call out as I throw my bag on the couch.

"In the kitchen!"

I head into what we call the kitchen, which is more like a closet where they stuck a stove, and smile as she hands me a glass of wine.

"You're the best."

"I know," she grins and then goes back to stirring something in the pot.

"What are you making?"

"Rice pudding. I figured it was time for some comfort dessert."

Rice pudding is Aunt Brenna's famous recipe. She makes it every year for the holidays and always give us some to bring back.

"So, if you're making rice pudding, I'm going to assume we have a crisis?"

She shrugs. "You can be dramatic when it comes to your nemesis. I'm just prepared for it."

I'm not dramatic. That's the thing of it, I am so under dramatic about him it's crazy. Instead of pitching a fit, like I've wanted to, I've been calm and used his superiority against him to stay at the top of my game.

And I don't actually think he's superior. He's just a major ass.

It doesn't help that our families have met and my Uncle Sean is friends with his dad. I have to hear that shit all the time too. They apparently came up in the minor leagues or some crap.

I don't know.

And of course, Cayden's twin brother is the starting second baseman for the Yankees, so my other cousin, Austin, always bitches about him. The Benson-Hennington name is constantly uttered around me, as though I need any more reminders of him.

My point is, I don't flip out, I just…loathe him.

"I'll take the rice pudding without the commentary," I tell her.

Melanie grins. "We know that's not going to happen. Now, spill the tea."

I run through my meeting with him and then the visit in my office. As I sip my wine and tell the story, I feel a little better at how I handled things.

"I'm surprised it ended that way," Mel says as she turns off the burner and puts the lid on the pot.

"Why?"

"Because I would've expected him to follow you home or be outside the office with cupcakes or flowers. He's smooth and calculating, he doesn't give up either. I just can't imagine he went home after you denied him access to the building like a kicked puppy."

"I thought the same thing. I was so prepared to walk to the subway with my headphones in, ignoring him the entire way."

Not that anyone ever really ignores him. He's hard to miss and even harder not to look at. Cayden is sexy beyond words. He's tall with light brown hair, and when he looks at you, the world falls away around him.

I really hate that part.

Melanie drains her wine before filling us both up. "Does his case have legs?"

"Not really. Whoever drew up the contract before left me a lot of wiggle room and I plan to take all of it."

"So, his clients signed it and yours won't?"

"The contract is signed, but when Cayden took over handling the case, he found the errors and is trying for a renegotiation since no monies have been transferred. I guess it's what I would do."

She raises her glass. "Then we know it's the right move."

I smile, loving how my cousin always has my back. "But it's not for my clients. Their error works in my benefit."

"Then you give him hell, my friend." Melanie raises her wine glass and I clink mine.

The two of us sit on the floor of the living room, eating takeout, drinking wine, and talking. Her life is so much more glamourous than mine. She's doing amazing things in the fashion industry and gets to meet some incredible people. Her mentor is getting ready to launch a new fall line and Melanie got to design a subset that will be premiered.

"Are you nervous?" I ask.

"I'm literally down eight pounds because I can't eat."

I snort. "Hence the need for rice pudding?"

"Crap!" She hops up and goes to the stove, removing the cover. "Thank God you said something!"

Mel starts grabbing things out of the fridge and there's a knock at the door.

"Shit!" I say under my breath. "The doorman must've let Uncle Dec in."

Melanie laughs and jerks her head. "He loves us."

"He's here because of my father."

"And mine. Lord knows they think we're both still little girls."

My family is a bunch of crazy, amazing people. My dad has three brothers, Declan, Sean, and Jacob, who is Melanie's stepfather. We grew up all living on the same farm, having ridiculous Saturday night bonfires, Sunday brunches that were filled with amazing food, and a closeness I never knew was possible.

However, it also comes with the most overprotective bunch of maniacs that have ever lived. Especially when it comes to their daughters and nieces.

I open the door with a smile. "Hi, Uncle De—"

The name dies on my tongue because it's not my uncle standing there—it's Cayden Benson-Hennington.

Chapter Four

CAYDEN

Coming here was a risk, but after running across the street, getting her a coffee and flowers and waiting outside her building for two fucking hours, I asked the security guard to call up again and he smirked, letting me know she left already.

"Who let you in?" Hadley asks through gritted teeth.

"Your very kind doorman who was thrilled because I come bearing gifts…a peace offering of sorts."

I hold up the coffee, that's completely ice cold, and isn't safe to drink, and the flowers that are now in desperate need of water.

She eyes the cup. "What are you *really* doing here?"

"I explained, I come in peace."

"There is no peace with you."

I let out a quick chuckle. "That's true. But regardless, I stopped by the office, waited there for hours while you had already left, so I didn't want the flowers and coffee to go to waste."

Her arms cross right under her breasts, pushing them up just a bit. *Eyes up, Hennington.* "You bought the coffee hours ago?"

"I did, but in my defense, I would've been here sooner if I didn't have to bribe someone from your office to give me your address after realizing you ghosted me."

"That's a breach of privacy, so thanks to them," she huffs.

"I'm very persuasive."

"I bet you are. Also, I didn't ghost you since I never was supposed to even see you."

Little does she know there was no breach from her office. I called my brother, asked him to call Sean Arrowood, saying she forgot her credit card with me from lunch, and that's how I got it. I don't plan to tell her that though.

A beautiful girl with red hair and freckles splattered across her face comes to the door. "You must be Cayden."

"I am."

She flashes a dazzling smile. I know many guys who would fall at her feet, but my gaze doesn't linger long. Instead, my eyes go back to Hadley with her soft brown hair the shade of coffee or mocha, and those eyes. Those fucking green eyes that are impossible to forget. No matter how much I've tried.

"I'm Melanie." the redhead extends her hand.

I flash my signature smile and return the gesture. "It's nice to meet you."

Hadley makes a gagging noise. "Don't fall for it, Mel. That smile has felled many women."

"You would know," Melanie says under her breath, but not low enough I didn't catch it.

"So, you talk about me?" I ask a little playful, but also curious.

"Only what an ass you are and how you think your shit doesn't stink."

"I never said that, and I'm not an ass. If I were, I wouldn't come here with flowers and coffee. I would've just annihilated you in negotiations rather than try to work it out like adults."

Hadley shakes her head. "You forget, I know you, Cay. I know your tricks and your charms."

"All I keep hearing is that you think I'm charming."

"I recall the word was ass."

Melanie's eyes volley back and forth as we bicker. "You know what?" Her cousin claps her hands and we both turn to her. "I just remembered that I have to go to work and fix a few patterns before the seamstresses get in."

"Tonight?" Hadley asks.

"Yeah, I meant to do it before I left and…just totally slipped my mind."

Hadley's eyes narrow and she speaks through a fake smile. "Can't you go tomorrow?"

"Nope. It's super important. You wouldn't want me to mess up the line, would you?" Melanie turns to me. "It was great meeting you, Cayden. You are everything I hoped you'd be."

Not sure what that means, but her leaving is clearly making Hadley uncomfortable, and while my goal isn't that, it should make the negotiation a little easier if she's off her game.

"The pleasure is all mine." I lay it on thick by grabbing her hand and kissing the top of it.

"Oh, please!" Hadley grumbles.

Melanie laughs, seemingly immune to my game. She leans in to where Hadley can't hear. "A little less on the asshole and more on the fun with that one."

"Thanks for the tip."

She pats my chest. "Good luck."

"Traitor," Hadley mutters as Melanie grabs her purse and heads out the door.

After she leaves, Hadley and I stand there, in the awkward silence. It's a good thing I planned ahead a little bit.

"Did you eat yet?"

She shakes her head. "Not really."

"Good."

I take a step back into the hallway, and grab part two of my plan. Pizza.

There is nothing in the world that makes this woman happier than pizza. I happen to know this as we shared many of them in college and working on cases when we were both interns.

She eyes the box dubiously. "This is your plan?"

"Do you have whiskey?"

Her eyes sparkle with what I hope are memories of the past and she shakes her head. "Whiskey is a mistake."

"Whiskey is never a mistake."

"Come in, I can never turn down pizza and I'll grab the bottle."

That was what I was hoping for.

* * * *

"Take a shot!" she says as her head falls back on the seat of the couch.

"I didn't lose."

"You didn't win! You have to take a shot."

I have had *way* too much to drink and Hadley can barely hold her head up, but it's been the best night I've had in a very long time.

We ate pizza, talked about college and the time that she beat me in a debate in class. One that I should've won, but Professor Stein was moody and didn't think my argument contained passion and depth.

I don't know what that mattered since I was right.

"You didn't beat me," I say, my mouth feeling hard to move. "You take the shot."

Hadley picks up the glass and knocks it back. "Don't be a pussy. You lost—pay the price."

I rise to the bait, not willing to let her win, and fill my glass, keeping my eyes on her the whole time and let the liquid slide down my throat, burning the whole way.

I cough and Hadley bursts out laughing.

My laughter follows and I shake my head. "We're both plastered."

She lifts the bottle, turning her head to the side to look at it. "We are."

"Last time we drank this much we had amazing sex," I lean against the coffee table, resting my head on my hand. I have a very heavy head.

"You're giving yourself a lot of credit there, Hennington. I never said it was amazing."

My ego is instantly bruised. "Really?"

"It was decent."

"Decent?" I ask, no longer feeling too drunk.

She giggles and grabs her full shot glass, tossing it back. Her long brown hair is coming out of her knot thing on her head, her throat exposed, creating a long line as she gulps the liquid down. I am transfixed on her neck, and the soft skin there that I want to run my tongue down.

This is bad. We need to stop.

I grab the bottle, putting it behind me. "No more whiskey."

Her lips turn into the most adorable pout. "You're no fun."

"I'm a lot of fun."

She scoffs. "Please. You spent all of college doing what?"

"The same thing as you!"

"Exactly. No fun. We studied. We prepared for real life. We didn't do anything adventurous or reckless."

I've had enough reckless in my life. I have seen the consequences of being reckless. My biological father killed himself when I was ten years old. My brother and I were down in the living room, playing video games, which he told us to do, and then fifteen minutes later, our lives were no longer the same.

Mom came home, found him dead, and then the world imploded around us.

He lost all our money being reckless. He left us with debt, no answers, and heartache for a lifetime.

So, no, I don't do things that are reckless. I work hard, I save my money, and I am extremely careful with my emotions.

Except with Hadley.

She's the only person who I ever lose control around.

Like now.

"I think we are in a much better place than the people who made stupid decisions," I counter.

"Maybe, but maybe not. This is the most irresponsible thing I've done in two years."

"Get drunk?"

She nods. "Well, get drunk with you. The guy I can't seem to hate enough."

That gets through my drunken fog. "Why do you hate me? I'm lovable."

"That's the issue!" Hadley says and then burps. "See! I am a mess around you. I want to hate you so much, but then I think about your lips and your face and your hands and...damn it, I need to shut up."

"I think about you too." The words slip out before I have a chance to stop them.

Hadley's eyes find mine. "We shouldn't think about each other."

"No, we probably shouldn't."

"Confession... I think about that night. I remember it all. You're the last man I slept with."

It rocks through me. My heart, my head, and my cock love the confession far too much. Hadley is stunning, even drunk, hair falling out of her messy ponytail and sweatshirt falling off her shoulder. If anything, she's even more beautiful because she's not polished.

I move around the coffee table that separates us and bring my hand to her cheek, brushing the soft skin there with my thumb. "Confession...when I'm alone and jerking off, it's always you I think about, and right now, I want to strip you down and make you scream my name, so I have a new memory to think about."

"We probably shouldn't do that."

"We definitely shouldn't do that."

She shifts her body towards me, hand wrapping around my wrist, and leans in. "But I'm tired of doing the right thing."

Her lips are on mine a second later, and I don't care much about what we shouldn't do either.

Chapter Five

HADLEY

Why does this man make me crazy?

Why did I practically throw myself in his arms?

Because I'm an idiot. A drunk one. But even sober, I want this.

I want him. The only stupid man in a city of almost nine million that I dream of.

Maybe it's because of all the reasons I shouldn't. Maybe this is some daddy issue I don't even know I have. Whatever the reason is, I am just drunk enough not to care.

Cayden's tongue pushes into my mouth, his hands guiding my head to the side so he can kiss me harder, deeper, controlling the kiss.

I wrap my arms around his neck, loving the way his body feels against mine.

He moves his lips down my neck, to where my shoulder is exposed. "You skin is so soft," he murmurs before running his tongue back up the way he kissed and then circling the shell of my ear. "So sweet too. Are you still sweet other places, Hadley?"

My eyes close as his words wash over me. "Maybe you should find out," I counter.

"I will but you're going to have to ask me nicely."

"No."

"No?" Cayden asks as he nips my ear.

"No. I'm not going to ask you nicely."

I can feel the grin against my skin. "We'll see about that."

This is what we get off on. The part of me that only he understands. I want to fight. I want to push him, have him push me back, and argue until we both get what we want.

"Yes, I guess we will." I pull his face back so I can look into his eyes. They're warm, liquid, and swimming with desire. "Kiss me."

"Please…" he prompts.

He's out of his fucking mind. I'm not going to say please. Instead, I press my lips to his, moving my hand down at the same time, brushing his rock-hard cock. That touch causes a slip in his control. His mouth opens to me, and I take the lead. Our tongues slide against each other and when I rub a little harder, Cayden moans.

When he confessed to thinking of me when he touches himself, I thought I might die. The images that came to me were so intense, and I want to see it for myself. Which if I were sober, I would never admit.

His fingers slide against my spine, and then move between us, finding bare skin against my stomach.

When I got home, I changed into my normal staying in attire. A baggy sweatshirt, shorts, and a messy bun. Right now, I'm pretty grateful for the lack of undergarments and things that would definitely make it harder for him to touch me.

Cayden's hand moves higher, finding my breast. He kneads the right one and runs a finger around my nipple. He breaks the kiss but pulls my lower lip in his teeth as he pulls back. "I bet you're sweet here."

"I couldn't tell you."

"Do you want to know, love?"

The instinct to argue is so high, but I want it. I want his tongue and mouth there. I want him to kiss me and I can fight it or give in this time. Deciding that there's a middle ground is where I land. "Only if you do."

He chuckles. "Well played. I definitely do. I already told you that."

"Then maybe you should shut up and do what we both want."

"So you do want it. I knew you'd admit it."

Damn him.

"I hate you."

"You only wish you did," Cayden's voice is low as he moves his head towards my breast. "You wish you didn't want my mouth on your body. You wish you could hate me and not want me, and do you know how I know this?"

My head falls back as the heat of his mouth draws closer. "No," I let the word fall out, answering his question.

"Because I feel the same."

I can't respond because the sensations become too much. His tongue slides around my nipple, flicking it back and forth slowly as his hands caress my breasts. I feel lightheaded, and not just from the alcohol.

Somewhere between his kiss and our bickering, I lost some of the buzz I was enjoying so much.

Now the only thing I feel is him.

His lips. His tongue. His hands.

All of it is surrounding me, wrapping me like a blanket and warming every inch of my body.

"Cayden," I moan his name as he moves to the other side.

He does the same again and my fingers fist in his dark brown hair.

When he pulls back, he quickly grabs me, lifting me as though I weigh nothing and placing me on the couch. My sweatshirt is gone a second later and he pushes my legs apart.

"Are you ready to say please?" he asks before pressing a kiss to the inside of my knee.

The defiance in me rises. There's no way. I will not beg him.

I shake my head.

Cayden tsks and then his hands move up my thighs. "Such a shame. If you ask nicely, I'll pull these shorts off and run my tongue up your legs until I find your sweet pussy."

Don't do it. Don't give in. The game will be over and that will be that.

"Since you want it, you should ask me nicely," I try to keep the desperation out of my voice because I want it so bad.

So damn bad.

His smirk tells me I didn't succeed. He pushes up on his knees, moving towards me and starts unbuttoning his shirt. I watch as his fingers move slowly and I can feel his gaze on me. "I never denied I want it, Hadley. I never said I didn't want you. I ache for you, love. I think of your defiant mouth wrapped around my dick. I imagine your taste, your moans, your perfect body, and what your face will look like when I'm buried inside of you." The shirt falls off and I want to weep.

Cayden's body is ridiculous. The thick muscles that hide beneath his shirt are sinful. I know what a farmer's body can look like, the way the years of manual work take the place of the gym. But we haven't been on our farms in years. However, you'd never know looking at him now.

He moves even closer to me, his lips just barely brushing against mine. "I can't do it," I admit.

What Cayden doesn't know is that while I have an amazing father now, I didn't as a child. I can't beg him. For years I watched who I believed to be my father beat my mother, make her beg for her life, for my safety. Kevin beat my mother within an inch of her life, all while she pleaded for him to stop. If it weren't for her bravery, I would be dead.

And if it weren't for my father, so would she.

I promised myself that I would never beg a man for anything.

Cayden brushes his fingers along my chin. His eyes studying mine. I see the understanding in his green eyes. Then another emotion, one I can't name takes its place. "Who hurt you?" his voice is calm, but a trace of anger lingers.

"I can't."

"I won't ever hurt you, Hadley. I...won't."

"I know."

And I do. I trust this infuriating man. He and I have battled so many times and it has never been because he wants to hurt me. Cayden comes from the same place of needing to win, and I understand him more than I care to admit.

I takes his face in my hands, worried he'll want to talk about the shit in my past I work hard to forget. "I won't beg, but I will ask this—if you want me, show me."

His eyes close and he moves forward in a heartbeat. His lips are on mine, kissing me like a starving man tasting food for the first time.

My fingers thread in his thick hair, holding him there, kissing him back and pouring all my desire in it. I want him so bad. I hate that I want him so bad, but I do.

I hate that the alcohol has taken away the resistance I worked so hard to build.

Cayden pulls back, his hand moving to my hips and pulling at the shorts. I lift my hips to help him and then they're gone. I'm buck ass naked in the middle of the living room.

This is so stupid.

But before I can protest or state that this is a bad idea since my cousin could walk in at any minute, his hands are spreading my thighs apart and I feel his tongue make a glorious swipe against my clit.

Yeah, I'm not saying a damn word to stop him now.

Cayden doesn't ask me to either. He just licks and makes circles in all the right places. My heart is pounding so hard the echo of the pulse in my ears drowns out everything around me. I let my eyes close, the sensations overwhelming me as I climb faster than I ever have on my own towards an orgasm.

He moves my hand to the back of his head and I guide him to the left a little. "Yes," I gasp when he hits the perfect spot again. "Yes, there. Oh, Cayden."

His tongue presses harder and I move on instinct, but he holds my hips down and spreads my legs apart even more.

I'm at his mercy. I can't go anywhere and I'm forced to endure and also enjoy his mouth.

I start to pant harder, my breathing ragged as I move closer. Then, before I even know it, I'm falling apart, screaming out his name over and over. I have never orgasmed so fast in all my life. I was chasing it and then before I knew it, I was gone.

He lifts his head, kissing my stomach, my leg, and then my other one. "You're as sweet as I hoped. Sweeter than I remember. I'm not asking you to beg, but I want to ask if you want more?"

My emotions shift from overwhelming joy to gratitude. "I want it all."

"Thank fucking God."

He stands, removing his pants and I giggle when they get stuck around his ankles. We both laugh as, in my attempt to help, I fall off the couch and can't manage to get my limbs to work to get back up.

Cayden lowers himself beside me on the floor and then pulls me on top of him.

I straddle his hips, looking down at him.

He looks up at me. "I really fucking hope you don't regret this tomorrow."

I shake my head. "I won't."

"Then I hope you remember."

I adjust myself so the tip of his cock is right at my entrance. His eyes close as I start to take him in. The feeling of him filling me is so intense I could weep. It's heaven and hell and all the places in between.

He offers me pleasure but I also know this will never happen again. It can't. We are opposing counsel and will always be enemies in some way.

When I lift up, taking him fully, I feel my muscles clench as pleasure becomes intense again.

"Fuck," he groans. "God you were made for me."

Right now, it feels like he was made for me as well, but we can't be.

I wait, unmoving until his gaze meets mine. "This can't happen again."

"I know. So, fuck me tonight so that I can relive it tomorrow."

And I do.

I ride him so hard that I will remember it always.

Chapter Six

HADLEY

"Hi there, handsome. You miss me? I'm sorry I didn't come give you love sooner," I say, petting his long nose. Max snorts, lifting his head a few times and then settles it on my shoulder. "I'm sorry, I won't wait so long next time."

He stomps his hoof and I smile. Max has been my horse the last eleven years. He was a foal that came from Aunt Devney's mare and I fell in love with him instantly. By the grace of God, I was able to convince my parents to board him in New York so I could come see him. I'm still not sure how Dad went for it. I searched for somewhere close to the city, but one that also would allow him to have room to roam and wasn't so expensive they could refuse me.

I found a small, family-owned stable on Long Island. It's a bit farther than I would've liked, but it's not like New York City is brimming with farms. This was close to feeling like home where I could get to him easily by train.

"He's doing well," A voice says from behind me. Vicky, the stable master smiles as she walks towards us.

I give his nose another rub. "He looks good."

"We exercised him a bit yesterday. He was stomping around, clearly missing you."

I shake my head. "You were lonely, Max? I'm sorry, buddy. I know it's been a few weeks. Forgive me?"

He turns his head to the side and I laugh.

"Such a man," Vicky says.

"Is he eating okay?"

"He is now. I think the difference in hay was upsetting him, but he's acclimated to it well."

A few weeks ago, Max was refusing to graze. I was worried about bloat, but thankfully Vicky and her staff were already on it and had the vet out. Everything looked okay, but we increased his activity with the pen walker and adjusted how much grain over hay he was getting.

"Good. I'm going to ride him today."

She nods. "He'll appreciate that. Won't you, boy?"

He does his grumble and I sigh. "You're so dramatic, Max."

"You know boys, they want to be ridden."

My face flushes as I remember the man I rode quite hard yesterday. God, I was a dummy. After we finished, I lied on the floor in his arms and I realized not only did we have sex, but we did so without a condom.

Thank God for the pill.

"You okay?" She asks.

"I'm fine. Sorry, just spaced out there."

"I better check on our newcomer. Stop by the last stable on the left before you go. She's beautiful and she'll be here for the birth of her foal."

"Oh! Definitely! I got to watch this guy be born and it was the most amazing thing."

Vicky nods. "It's an unforgettable experience. We're guessing she has another week, but her owner passed away and her daughter had no idea, just that she couldn't get her mother's affairs in order and deal with a pregnant horse."

"How awful. I'll definitely stop by."

She heads off to do her never-ending list of chores and I grab my saddle, needing a mental break.

Mel got home yesterday about two hours after we finished and smirked at me when she saw the living room. This morning I left before she woke up and could ask me a million questions I didn't want to answer.

Once Max is saddled, he's moving around a lot, shifting so I can't mount. "What's going on, huh?" He moves again and I check the straps. "Is it too much or are you still prickly about me not coming last week?" As though he's going to answer. However, I have always been like this with my horses. I talk, they listen, and I pretend they understand and answer. I am who I am. "I'm sorry about that, Max. I've been super busy at work and when I brought you here, we discussed this. If it's because I'm a little off today, well, that's not all my fault. You see, last night, that stupid man came to my house, we drank too much, clothes came off, and well, I'm a mess. But I'm here and I love you and I think we both need to ride so will you let me get up now?"

Max, the brooding beast, shifts again to the left. I groan.

"You know they can sense your mood?" A voice I know says from behind me. I close my eyes, really not wanting or needing to see him today.

There is no reason that Cayden Benson-Hennington should be in my happy place.

"What, are you stalking me now?"

He laughs. "No."

"Then why the hell are you at a stable on Long Island?" I ask, turning to face him.

Mistake. Big one.

In a suit, Cayden is gorgeous. Absolutely freaking amazing.

In tight jeans and a cowboy hat…dear God. I am screwed.

My jaw is slack, taking in the very country attire he's wearing, leaning against the entrance to the stables.

"Did you notice they have fifteen head of horse? You're not the only one who needed to ride today."

Of course. "You board your horse here?"

He nods. "I sure do."

"Seriously."

"It's a great place. Close to the city, has open fields, and a trail that won't spook my girl. I guess you felt the same, hence why your gelding is also here."

"Yes, clearly," I reply. I rub Max's neck, trying—and failing—to keep my eyes off Cayden's lower half.

"Anyway," Cayden says, pushing off the side and walking toward us. "I was saying he can sense your energy and it's clear you're agitated."

"I wasn't until about a minute ago."

"You're saying I'm your instigator?"

I sigh. "Yes."

Cayden laughs. "I don't think so, but if you need to tell yourself that, go ahead."

My head is not in the right place for this today. "I speak the truth, but as much as I would love to continue this, I came here to ride."

Cayden looks to Max, who normally looks away from strangers, but is studying him. "Hey there, big boy. You're a handsome guy."

Max is a beautiful horse. He would've been an amazing stud, but we weren't in a position to breed him.

"He doesn't like strangers," I warn Cayden.

"He seems to like me. As I said before, I'm pretty lovable."

I roll my eyes. "Not to Max. He's an excellent judge of—" I start to say more but my very non-trusting and anti-men horse brushes his nose to Cayden's outstretched hand.

"Character? I agree. He knows I'm safe and I'm a horse guy."

Yes, I remember. Cayden's family owns a horse farm, which is where I got my first horse from. I loved her so much. She is now almost twenty-four and lives the good life in the fields at home.

However, Max doesn't know this and is supposed to be rude to him because I will it so.

"Traitor," I whisper to him.

He doesn't seem to care, just allows Cayden to pet him.

"As much as I'd love to stay here, I have a limited amount of time before I need to head home. Come on, Max, we're going to ride now."

"I'm saddling up Sadie, how about we ride together?"

"I'd rather not. I need time with Max so he'll forgive me."

Cayden smirks. "Afraid?"

"Of what?"

"Being alone with me again?"

Oh, please. "Not even a little bit."

"Then let me saddle her up and go out with you."

I huff. "Why? We don't even really like each other."

"I think we disproved that last night. Or, at least, I showed you that I don't dislike you at all," he admits. "I like you a lot. I like you more than I should and I came here to stop thinking about how much I fucking like you and then I find you here."

Why do I like that? Why does his admission make me want to kiss him? Because I'm a nincompoop. That's why.

"If you know me at all, it's not hard to figure out I'm either here or I'm at work," I try to sound blasé about it, not wanting him to see how much I like that he found me.

I like that our lives are entwined again in some way.

And also wanting to fight against the like. "I'm leaving now. If you catch up, I guess we'll ride together."

I grab the bridle, give Max a stern look that says *do not ruin my dramatic exit*, and hop up, leaving Cayden behind and hoping he follows.

Chapter Seven

CAYDEN

I don't saddle Sadie. There's no need, I can ride bareback better than saddled anyway. There are four possible trails Hadley could've taken, and I have no clue which one she would go on. My gut says follow the harder one, because she would want me to not think she went that way, but then I wonder if she wouldn't take the beginner one, thinking I would think she is on the advanced one.

Then, there are the two in the middle.

I adjust my balance, holding Sadie's mane. "Which way girl? Where did she go? Show me the way."

I give her the reins and she goes to the path in the middle. Neither of those are what I would've chosen.

But as we move through the trees, I see Hadley, her back straight, head lifted toward the sky, and hands out to the side—not even holding Max's reins as he walks along.

The trust between those two is fucking breathtaking.

I know it well. My horse Superman and I were that way. I didn't even have to think, he would just move the way I needed.

Sadie is a great mare, but nothing like the bond I had with my first horse.

I move carefully, not wanting to spook her or Max while she doesn't have control. I clear my throat and pull Sadie back a little. Hadley turns, her eyes flashing with surprise and then her head falls back.

I grin and make my way toward her. "Found you, Cowgirl."

"I am not a cowgirl."

I shrug. "It's what my stepdad calls my mom, guess it stuck."

"That's what he calls her?"

"It's his nickname for her. My mom was a cowgirl through and through."

"I guess growing up in Tennessee would do that."

I laugh. "She barrel raced, can rope better than most ranch hands, and helps on our farm."

"My mother never wanted to run a farm, but Arrowood Farms kind of negated her hopes there," Hadley smiles and my chest tightens. "I love it. I loved getting up in the morning, helping with the chores, and then at night I got to ride."

When she's like this, unguarded and open, it's hard to breathe. If she knew half of what she does to me, she'd own my world and I can't have that. Not when I need her to concede on the case so I have a world left.

While I never expected to find her here today, I need to make up for the complete fuck up that was last night. I never should've got drunk, slept with her, and said things she didn't need to know…all of that was a mistake. All of that was not part of the plan.

Now I need to get back to that plan.

"See how much we are the same?"

She raises a brow at that. "Because we both grew up on a farm?"

"And now we're both lawyers. I know it's cold there in my shadow, but you're not bad."

"Not bad?" Her voice rises. "I am ten times better than you think. I should've beaten you at every turn, but you're just a better liar than I am."

"I think you meant to say lawyer. I am a better lawyer than you are. Which is why I won and you didn't."

She shakes her head, huffing. "You're such an asshole."

"Never denied that, sweetheart."

"Don't call me that. I am not your sweetheart, love, babe, sugar, any of that. Got it?"

I raise my hands. "I hear you loud and clear."

Her green eyes go to my legs. "Really? Bareback?"

"You had a head start. I use my advantages where I can."

"What do you want, Cayden? You want me to give you an out on the case? To say after a passionate mistake that you can screw my clients over after your associate made the mistake? Not going to happen."

I didn't think it would. "It would've been the generous thing to do."

"Yes, it would and I'm not that generous. Not when I have a career that I have to work ten times harder to be successful at. You're part of the good ol' boy club who got to pull case files and research, while I was fit to bring coffee and write reports during my internship."

"I brought just as much coffee as you," I remind her.

"Until you didn't."

And then, Hadley kicks Max's flanks and takes off at a trot. I let her go because while I'm great bareback, trotting is fucking painful, which she probably knows and why she did it.

"Come on Sadie, we'll find another way."

* * * *

When I get back to my apartment, I shower, grab an apple, and sit down to study this contract. As many times as I've looked at it, I feel like I'm missing something. Some loophole to work in my favor where we can back out of the deal without penalty.

As I'm reading through, my head swimming from the last twenty-four hours, my phone rings, flashing my twin brother's name.

"Hey fuckhead," I answer.

"What up, dickbag?"

"Working. You?"

Logan laughs. "It's the way we are. Which I am going to somehow manage to blame dad for."

"Which one?"

"Both," he says and I get it. Our father, the one who took his life, was a workaholic. He based his entire worth on that one thing, how good he was at investing. When it fell apart, he did as well. Then the man who raised us since, who we call dad as well, positioned the family horse ranch to become one of the top producers in the country. People from all over come to Hennington Horse Ranch because we have quality unsurpassed.

Hard work and dedication have been our motto since birth.

"How is the team looking?"

"Good. We're home this week so I thought we could grab a beer tonight."

Logan plays for the Yankees. He's that guy who everyone in this city loves. I can't go out on a game day and not see my brother's name plastered on the back of a jersey. Not that the Yankees put names on jerseys, but you know... Yankee fans are one of a kind.

He's become their second coming of Christ and I'm just lucky enough to have shared a womb with him, as he reminds me each time I bitch about the people in this town not seeing him as the prick he is.

"Can you do that?"

"What? Drink?"

"Leave your house with all the people who love you. I mean, it's dangerous, Lo. You could be attacked by a rabid fan who wants to have your babies." I say, as though I'm horrified and worried.

"Fuck off."

I chuckle. "I'm only sort of kidding."

"Look, fans know better when we're home. It's why I love being in New York. We get to live a little. It's when we're in Boston that I want to crawl in a hole and hide."

"It's so hard being you," I toss at him.

"It's really not."

"Asshole."

"That you love," he reminds me. "Now, want to meet me in Chinatown or SoHo?"

SoHo is where Hadley is. I need to avoid SoHo so that I don't end up running into her again. Not until I have this case figured out. "Chinatown is fine. We can hit up that restaurant we went to last time."

"All right. I'll meet you there at six."

"See you then."

Chapter Eight

CAYDEN

I should've known better than to come out with Logan. Anyone with a sibling knows they're a pain in the ass sometimes, anyone with a twin knows they're doubly so. As soon as we sit down his eyes narrow and he laughs.

"What?"

"You're all hung up on some girl."

"I'm not hung up on anything. And what the fuck does that even mean?"

"You look like shit, first off. Second, you didn't deny it which means I'm right," he leans back, arms crossed with a stupid grin I'd like to run my fist into.

"And here I thought we might have a nice dinner. We haven't even ordered and you've managed to piss me off."

He shrugs. "It's a gift."

"Sure it is."

I take a second, because as much as Logan is a shithead, he's also someone who likes to keep the attention off himself only when there's something he doesn't want to discuss. So, the fact that he came at me first means he's worried I'm going to see that something.

"What's her name?" I ask as he stares over the menu.

"Who?"

"The girls that you're fucked up over?"

"There is no girl."

I raise a brow. "Interesting. There's always a girl."

My brother is a lot like our mother in some ways. When he falls, he falls hard. History has that way of repeating itself and my mother and father watched Logan with concern. He started dating Callista Hawthorne when we were in high school. Sure enough, they fell in love, which baffled me because Callie was a bitch if you asked anyone.

I digress.

They loved each other, had all these plans, she went to college in Ohio with him and when Logan got drafted, she lost her fucking mind.

Full blown, next level crazy shit. For the first time in my life, I saw my brother truly devastated. He loved her so much he almost walked away from baseball.

Since then, he refuses to love, just screws around to avoid that kind of pain.

"We're talking about you and your girl." He grins with his head tilted.

I narrow my eyes, and then I know I have him. "You saw Callista."

Maybe someone else would've missed his cue, but I know him way too well. He laughs and looks down at his menu. "Don't be stupid."

"Don't lie to me."

He sighs. "Fine. I saw her when we were in Tampa. She knew the Yankees were coming, sent me an email, and asked to have dinner."

Logan is so damn predictable. Of course he'd meet her, even after the theatrics, the threats, and her last ditch effort of claiming she was pregnant—which she wasn't.

"Let me guess, she's sorry, she was just upset and scared, she didn't mean to try to trap you into marriage…am I warm?"

"She's engaged."

I didn't see that one. "Oh."

"She's happy and… I don't know."

He looks like someone just punched him in the stomach. "Why aren't you happy about this? She moved on and, let's be honest, she had that whole *Terms of Endearment* thing going on."

"I loved her. No matter what you and Mom and Dad and pretty much everyone else thought of her… I loved her. If it all hadn't gone down the way it did, I would've married her, Cay. I," he pauses and I know my baby brother enough to hear the pain underneath it.

"You still love her."

"I don't even know who she is now. She's living in a small home, that her and her fiancé are renovating. They flipped their first house six months ago and are working on this one. She learned how to hang drywall and…you know, that wasn't her."

I snort. "No, that girl tried to pretend she was living in Manhattan, not Bell Buckle."

The waitress comes over and we place our orders. Once she's gone, I get back to the conversation because it keeps it off me and Hadley.

"So, seeing her brought back unresolved shit?"

"More like, I won't have that. I'm not unhappy with my life. Who the fuck would be? I'm literally making millions of dollars to play baseball every day. I could bang any girl I wanted, I'm pretty fucking good looking, and have nothing to complain about."

And then I hear our mom. "But you have no one to share it with."

He sighs heavily. "I swear, you sounded just like her and Dad."

"Because we heard that crap all the time."

My parents are ridiculously happy together. Zach and Mom were high school sweethearts. She followed him to college, and when Zach got drafted, their relationship fell apart. Mom moved on, married my dad, was happy and all that, until my father's death. Then, we lost everything and had to move to Tennessee. When we got there, they saw each other, planets shifted and stars aligned. Same old story about finding each other after all that time, and now they get to share their lives together, which is what matters.

"We did. And I keep wondering, how the hell am I ever going to meet someone who isn't after Logan the baseball player, millionaire, and celebrity, and actually gives a shit about Logan the man? Anyway, I told you my deep shit for the night, what's going on with you?"

I am so not telling him. "Not a thing."

"Lying son-of-a-bitch. You may be able to lie for a living, but I'm not buying it. Something is up."

"Nothing. I'm working on a case that has me a little irritated. Other than that, nothing to report."

Thankfully, the waitress appears with our beer and food at that moment, which might just save me from this damn conversation I don't want to have.

We both fall silent, eating and drinking. The dim sum is fantastic, and I forget about Hadley, her smile, the way she rode off, and leaving me feeling even more confused on how I feel about her.

Instead, I focus on the good food, semi-decent company, and the fact that I went a whole hour without remembering her around my cock.

That's a win.

But now I'm remembering again.

"Have you gone riding lately?" Logan asks, breaking up the silence.

"Today, actually."

"Ha!" Logan claps his hands. "I knew something was off. You only ride when you're feeling lost. You only feel lost when you have feelings about something—or someone—you shouldn't."

"Why did I have to share a womb with such an idiot?"

"Ahh, yes, your way of avoiding difficult conversations is in full force. Come one, I spilled my drama, let's hear yours."

As much as I'm relentless, my brother is worse. When he wants something, he doesn't give up. I can lie, and try to weasel out of it, but then he'll come to my apartment tomorrow, hounding me, maybe even show up at my work, where he'll take centerstage because my office is chock full of Yankee fans who think my brother is a god.

Spoiler alert, he's not. He wet the bed until he was seven. What kind of god does that?

My point is that it'll be a nightmare and I'm already living one. Her name is Hadley Arrowood.

"I slept with Hadley," I blurt it out. Might as well just get it over with.

"Yeah, you did that in college."

"Last night, or maybe it was this morning, I don't know."

He leans back. "I thought she hated you."

"She does."

"So how the hell did you end up naked?"

I fill him in on the case, the attempt to get her to see my reasoning, and the stakes of closing the merger so I can work on the one I really want to be doing. The one I brought to the damn firm and now may have to sit on the sidelines.

Logan, for all his shortcomings, is my best friend. He is always there for me, and we may give each other crap, but at the end of the day, there is no one in the world I trust and admire more than him.

"Wow. So, your feelings for her have obviously not gone away."

"No."

I have wanted her since the day I saw her. I've made her be the enemy because it's so much easier than admitting how much I like her.

"Well, brother, it seems you have a problem. But the question is, what are you going to do about it?"

If I knew that, I wouldn't be a damn mess.

Chapter Nine

HADLEY

My feet are up on my desk as I stare out at the familiar skyline. Buildings of varying heights, creating a cutout in the sky that I love. While I lived most of my life on a farm, this city is where I feel the most like myself.

I chew on my pen cap, thinking about how in the last three days I have been very unlike myself.

I don't do random hookups. I don't get drunk and sleep with guys—well, at least with guys not named Cayden. I am the sensible one. The rule follower. I am not like Melanie who lives her life without regret. This is my worst trait and also sometimes my best one.

My plan today was to work from home until my meeting with Renee and Ben to discuss options on the case.

When I sat on the couch, however, I did not think about anything other than the fantastic sex I had there and then Cayden's face as I ran off during our ride.

That man makes me crazy and I hate it.

There's a knock on my door, but the person doesn't wait for me to respond, it opens and then clicks closed before I can get to my feet.

When I see who is there, my heart stops. "Cayden."

He doesn't say anything as he moves in the room. I'm on my feet a second later, not sure what exactly is happening, but then my face is in his hands before he gives me the most crushing kiss I've ever experienced.

I respond without pause. My mouth opening to him, and the kiss becomes harder, more intense. My hands roam his chest, loving the tensing of his muscles beneath my touch.

He pulls back, working hard to catch his breath. "I need you."

I feel the same. "We…"

"I need you, Hadley. I need you."

My heart is pounding and I want to deny him, but I have never heard the ache in his voice like I do now.

I move my hands to his cheeks, looking into his green eyes, trying to decipher what's hidden there. He's hurting, or something deeper, and for whatever reason, he's here and I want to take that pain from him.

Because I am a fool who happens to want so much more from him.

I could deny him, but that would also be denying myself. *Just one more time.* One more kiss. One more memory to hold onto. It can't hurt more than what is already happening.

Lie.

"I need you too," I admit. I have thought of him for days and while I wish it were different, I ache for him.

He groans and then his mouth is on mine again. The kiss is frantic, as though we both know we're chasing time and regrets. There's no laughter or silliness like when we were drunk. This is pure lust.

"I am going to fuck you on this desk. I'm going to make you want to scream out, but you won't be able to," he promises and then turns me so my back is to his front. "I'm going to hike up this pretty skirt." He does as promised, his hand sliding between my legs. "Pull your panties to the side so I can finger you while you imagine it's my cock."

I shiver, but grin because he's about to find out the flaw to that plan real soon. He pushes me down, my face against the cool wood, and I hold onto the edge. I have dreamed of this so many times.

Cayden's hands move higher and then I hear the hitch in his voice. "Bad girl you are."

"Why is that?" I ask as he moves his other hand down my back.

"Because you're not wearing any panties."

"No. I'm not."

He kicks my legs apart more. "Keep them like this, sweetheart."

"Or what?"

"Or you'll find out."

I like this game we play. The fight for dominance. Because with Cayden, it seems to be a flaw of mine, I shift, not obeying his command. He takes a step back, the loss of his heat is immediate.

"Cayden?"

"I told you not to move."

"And I don't take orders."

He returns and his voice is rough in my ear. "If I didn't love the sight of you like this, laid out on your desk, bare ass in the air, waiting for my touch, I'd leave right now. I'd walk out with you wet and wanting." He pushes his finger inside of me, the pleasure taking away my protest. "You want me too much, though. You have thought about me coming here and doing this very thing to you. To make you feel good again. To show you how much you live in my damn head like I'm in yours."

Heat fills my cheeks and I bite my lip to keep from saying anything.

Cayden twists his fingers, pushing deeper. "You like when I do this too. When I fuck you with my fingers. You're so wet, so hot, so fucking perfect. However, we don't have time to play games right now. Someone could walk in at any second, couldn't they?"

His words cause my muscles to contract and I swear, I am so turned on it's embarrassing. "Yes."

"And do you want me to fuck you, Hadley, on your desk?"

More than I want to breathe. "Yes."

"Good answer."

He withdraws his fingers and I fight the urge to cry out from the loss. But I hear him release his belt and then the slide of the zipper. Cayden is at my entrance a second later and he drives deep.

I gasp as he fills me, giving no time to acclimate to his size. He pulls back, slamming into me again. I hold the edge of the desk, knuckles turning white because if I don't, I might fly across the room from the force of his thrusts.

"I want you so much," he admits. "Ever since we were together that first time, I have thought of this. Of you and me. I've imagined you a million ways."

My legs are trembling as my orgasm builds with each word. "You're in my head too," I pant.

"You're like a drug. I had a taste and now I need more." He pulls out and then turns me to face him. Cayden lifts me on the desk, positioning me so my legs are spread open and my ass is at the edge.

He drops to his knees, licking a few times and I fall back, wanting to die right here. "Cayden, please."

"Please what?" he asks, and then sucks my clit in his mouth.

God, I don't even care that he's sort of making me beg. I want him too much to care.

"Please don't stop." I don't even care what he does, just as long as he doesn't stop.

He stands again, licking his lips. "A whole security team walking in here right now couldn't get me to stop."

I'm jerked forward and then he's inside of me again. We don't say anything else, our gazes never leave the other though. What started as just a straight up fuck changed. There's something more. Something deeper. The pace is no longer rushed, it's slower and more deliberate. I push my heels into his ass, trying to drive him faster, but he doesn't do it.

His hand moves to my face, running his finger down my cheek. "So beautiful."

No, he can't do this. "Fuck me, Cayden."

He shakes his head. "You like it more like this."

"I don't." I lie because the truth is too dangerous.

His pace doesn't change, he moves intentionally, eyes never moving from mine. I feel too much, see too much in the depths of his gaze. That part I could deal with, it's what I know he can see in mine. The want, desire, the feelings that for so long I have masked as anger and hatred, because it's so much easier than love and hope.

"I think you wish you didn't."

Before I can look away, my orgasm rocks through me, crashing over me in waves that leave me breathless and my lungs hurting.

He follows me over the edge, pulling me to his chest. I feel the tears coming and I can't stop them. I hate myself for this. I don't want to cry in front of him, but I feel so raw.

Damn it.

I clamp my jaw tight and do everything I can to push my feelings aside.

His thumb brushes against my temple and the beating of his heart pounds in my ear.

"That was…"

I lift my head as the shame and self-hatred starts to build. I'm in my office. I just had sex in my freaking office. I should've stayed home. God, what am I doing? I'm sleeping with opposing counsel, at work, and I have to review this case today. And then I start to wonder, what the hell is this?

What are we even doing?

Cayden has never shown even a glimmer of interest until now. When his case has issues, and there is no way he can beat me. Now, suddenly, he needs me?

Am I just some part of his game to mess with my head so he can find a way to get me to cave?

These questions swirl inside of me and the contentment of feeling connected leaves and is refueled by confusion and anger.

Inhaling deeply once, I push against his chest, "You have to go."

Cayden steps back, the loss of him feels like a punch, but I focus on cleaning up and trying to appear like I didn't just get fucked in my office.

"Hadley?"

"Get dressed and go, please."

He grips my arm as I start to walk away, knowing I have to spray perfume or something to get rid of the sex smell that lingers in here.

I look at the hand and then his face. "Let go of me."

He drops his grip immediately. "What is happening here?"

"You tell me."

"Well, from my perspective, we had incredible sex—again—and I have no idea what I did wrong. Why are you pushing me away?"

I am an intelligent girl. I have spent years learning to focus on being rational and communicating because half of what my job is just that. I have to keep emotions at bay and be logical. Right now, yeah, that's gone.

There are nothing but emotions swimming around me and I'm not quite sure which one is going to exit my mouth now.

It could be the needy girl, who wants to ask him to hold me.

It could be the sad part of me, who needs reassurance that this isn't just fucking.

It could be the angry girl, who believes I'm being used for a case.

Or it could be the stupid one, who asks him to come over later since Melanie is gone for a week and we do this all over again.

Please don't be the stupid one.

"Because I don't know what the hell we're doing. Why now? Why are you suddenly in my office at eleven in the morning and screwing me against my desk? Why did you come to my apartment the other day or the stables? Why now, Cayden?"

He runs his fingers through his dark brown hair. "I didn't even mean to come here today."

My heart falls to the pit of my stomach. "Right."

That's the only word I'm able to mutter.

"That came out wrong," he says quickly, taking a step toward me, but I step back. "I mean that I was in my office, going over the case, trying to imagine a way out of this, trying to think like you. If I could see your angle, maybe I could see a way to counter it. And then, I didn't see the case. I didn't imagine how you'd argue with me about it. I just saw you. I saw your face and your smile and the way your eyes get a little greener when you're happy. I heard your laugh and the way you say my name."

I shake my head, not wanting to hear all this. "You and I...we can't be a thing. We aren't built to be a thing. We are tinder and a matchstick that will burn the world down if we combine."

He moves quickly, holding my upper arms in his grip. "Then let's burn the fuck down."

He's not talking sense. "You can't go from zero to one hundred in two days. This isn't us. We don't like each other. You're bossy and an annoying know-it-all. I'm brilliant and no one sees it because I have tits. You probably like the Yankees because your brother plays for them. I am a Red Sox fan. I mean, that right there is reason enough. But seriously, this will never work. Not now. Not when we have to be professional, and I don't have the luxury of screwing up." Those stupid tears start to form, making his face blur. "So, please, I'm asking you to leave so I can pull myself together and do my damn job."

Cayden's hands move my face, holding it as though I'm a baby bird that's about to fly away. I can see him warring with what to say. "Of course. However, when this case is over, no matter the outcome, we're going to have a serious conversation."

By then, his feelings will have righted themselves and I can go back to hating him because it's so much easier than admitting I might love him.

"Sure. When the case is over."

He leans in slowly, and I want to protest. I wish I was strong enough to do it, but I am weak and allow him to give me the most tender and sweet kiss. One that I know has obliterated my heart, just like the look in his eyes as everything shifted on my desk.

Cayden pulls back, much too soon, grabs his suit jacket, winks, and leaves my office.

And I sink down to the floor and cry, because I can't hold back any longer.

Chapter Ten

HADLEY

"Ms. Arrowood, your next client is here. I've sent him back," Patti, the office receptionist says through the phone.

I look at my schedule, confused because I have a clear day for the most part. The only meeting I have is with Renee to go over possible options to get more money if we agree to give up a seat on the board.

Which, I actually think might be a better option. Once the company takes over, we have no idea if it'll be profitable, but the other side is that they will most likely destroy the farm that she's spent her whole life building.

I haven't heard from Cayden in four days. Four days of me trying to pull myself together and forget him. I've gone to the gym every day, giving a lot of extra energy hoping to sweat him out of my head. That hasn't worked. I've meditated, because my mother swears that always helps clear her head when she's struggling. I'm clearly not built for that. And then I have gone to the stables everyday this week. Not even Max has helped. If anything, it's worse because I think of him most there.

"Patti, I don't have any clients coming today."

Before she can respond, my door opens and my dad walks in.

"Well, I wouldn't call myself a client."

I smile, my heart feeling light and settled at the same time. "Daddy." Immediately I'm on my feet and moving toward him.

His strong arms wrap around me, and I sink into his chest. There is nothing in the world that makes me feel safer and more like myself than a hug from him. He squeezes me tight and then kisses the top of my head. "Hello, Squirt."

I smile, shaking my head. "I am twenty-six, not really a squirt anymore."

"You'll always be my little girl. Learn to accept this."

"Sure, Daddy. Why are you in the city? Mom never said anything about it."

He sighs. "Your uncle needed me to come look at the security setup with the new company he's acquiring. I figured it was a reason to see you and your mother was pretty adamant I do exactly that."

"I'm surprised she didn't tag along."

"Oh, she wanted to, but she can't with the school year coming to an end."

My mother is the best teacher in the world. I know everyone probably thinks their favorite is the best, but it's true here. She is that person that just emanates kindness. Her kids love her so much and always come back when they're in town.

"They're lucky to have her."

"We all are," Dad says without hesitation. No one in this world loves her more than him.

"So, you're here, do you…" I check my watch, seeing it's a little past one. "Want to grab lunch?"

"Lunch would be good. Pizza?"

"Are there any other food options?"

He shakes his head. "You are going to become a pizza one day."

"I can accept that."

Daddy laughs and I hook my arm around his. We leave and head a few blocks down to my favorite spot. It's one of those pizza places you'd walk right past because it's tucked in. Melanie and I stumbled in after it started pouring when we were walking home and it's now our most loved restaurant in the city.

Plus, it's pizza.

"So, what's happening with that big case of yours?" Dad asks as we sit down with a pie.

"Tomorrow, I have another round of negotiations." And another round of seeing Cayden.

"Are you going to win?"

I shrug. "I have a very strong argument and my clients are willing to concede on two things, which is the leverage I need. I don't think we'll need to budge on either, but if we do, neither hurt them."

"Sounds like you have a good plan," Dad praises.

"A plan is just that though, I need to get the other lawyer to see my way."

"You will."

My dad never doubts my ability, even when I don't see it the same. He is levelheaded, smart, and because he was a Navy SEAL, he can handle extremely stressful situations. You know, like falling in love with opposing counsel and sleeping with him multiple times when you absolutely shouldn't.

"Dad, can I ask you something?"

"Anything."

I grin. "How did you handle going into missions, knowing someone might get hurt or worse?"

He puts his slice down, wipes his hands, and releases a long sigh. "You don't really handle it. You don't even consider it if you can. Battle is not a place for doubt or feelings. It's when you rely on your training and instincts. It's no different than when you have to argue a case."

"That's the problem. I can't…separate them suddenly."

His eyes narrow and I have a feeling he is guessing there's a boy, but my father doesn't do boys with me. It doesn't matter my age or the fact I am a grown woman. I am still seven in his eyes, climbing up to the treehouse or playing Go Fish. When I *tried* to date Avery Gladstone in high school, my mother had to threaten to make him sleep in the barn.

We went to prom and at the end of the night, his father and mine stood at the front door, staring us down to ensure we didn't kiss.

Little did they know we totally made out in the bathroom at the prom and he touched a boob.

"Why can't you do that?"

"Because, my feelings are muddled."

He quietly grunts. "And this case, is it the people you're protecting or fighting?"

"No, it's the lawyer."

Dad's face falls and his chin falls to his chest. "Hadley, no. You know I am not rational with this shit. It's why you have your mother. She is able to see sense."

"Well, I need you to be a big boy and accept that I am a grown woman and I need you to help me not have feelings."

"Good fucking luck with that. I didn't want feelings with your mother and we see how well that turned out. Hell, look at every damn Arrowood in our family, brimming with unwanted feelings. I would really love it if you didn't have feelings because then I don't have to have them with this guy I don't even know and want to kill."

This was a mistake. "You are so dramatic, you know that?"

"When it comes to my kids, yup. I know I'm dramatic. You and Bethanne are my world. There is nothing I wouldn't do to protect you both."

"You can't protect us always, Dad."

"No, I can't. And I hate it."

I smile. He really is an amazing father. "So, how do I separate these unwanted feelings?"

"You shove them down so far you can't see them during the battle, and after it's over, you face them head-on. Because if I've learned anything, it's that they don't stay buried, no matter how hard you try."

That's what I was afraid of. I will never be rid of this…and I really need to be so I can stop thinking of Cayden every day.

Chapter Eleven

HADLEY

This is a mistake that I am not going to make.

I tell myself that and start to walk away, but before I get five steps from Cayden's apartment building, I hear him call my name.

"Hadley?"

Shit.

I turn and attempt my nonchalant smile. "Hey, Cayden. Funny seeing you here."

He looks at his building and then to me. "Other than the fact I live here."

"You do?" I play dumb, and from the look on his face, not very well.

"You've been here."

"Oh! I forgot about that."

He laughs. "Sure you did."

Maybe one of those manholes will blow and then I can fall in it and never come out. That would work for me right about now.

I watch as he moves towards me, like a predator stalking his prey, and that's pretty much what I am right now. I'm the dumb deer who wants some bark and he's the hunter that has me in his sights.

"I should go," I try to evade.

"Why are you here?"

Because I'm a dumb girl and wanted to see you.

"It's about the case."

"So, you are here to see me."

Yeah, that manhole is looking pretty nice.

I can keep lying, which I should be good at considering my career choice, or I can come clean.

I'll go with lying.

"No, I didn't say that. I was saying that we should discuss the case."

"Sure, we'll…talk about the case. Why don't you come upstairs with me so I can get my files?"

We both know that's not what we're going to end up doing upstairs, but that's why I came here. Because I have thought of nothing other than his mouth, his body, and the way I feel when he's inside of me.

"All right."

I never stood a chance. He took the shot, and I'm down for the count.

His apartment is nothing like I imagined. It's a little retro, a little modern, and filled with records. I walk over to the desk area that has hundreds of them. "I didn't know you were so big on music."

"My father was in love with jazz. Logan and I would sit at his feet while he would play his records for hours. I'm partial to the sound of vinyl. There's something pure and comforting about it."

"May I?" I ask, pointing to the crate.

"Of course."

I thumb through, admiring the collection that varies so much. There is jazz, which I expected, but also country, hip hop, and rock. Then, towards the back there is one that makes me laugh. "Spice Girls?"

Cayden chuckles. "My brother is an ass."

"He's a fan?"

"Probably and this is his way to irritate me. Logan's thing is finding a record store when he's on the road. He'll pick up something he thinks I would like."

I like that they have that. I keep looking and then I feel him behind me. His breath on my neck, but that's it. I try to focus on the sleeves, looking at the various artists, but I can't concentrate.

Not when all I want is to feel his hands on my body.

This is stupid. I know it. I shouldn't have come here and I definitely shouldn't have accepted his invitation, but I wanted him too much to walk away.

"Pull that one out," his voice is rough and low against my ear.

I shiver as I feel just the slightest brush of his lips down my neck. "This one?" I ask because I honestly have no idea what one I was even looking at.

His hands reach from behind me, taking the record he wanted, his heat cocooning me as his chest is against my back.

This is just like my office all over again. The energy is changing and I can feel his erection as he moves even closer.

"This record is one of my favorites." My eyes close when his other hand wraps around my stomach, holding me in place. "I love the beat of the song, the way the bass hits in varying speeds. I've always wanted to listen to it with you."

"Why?" I manage to get the single word out.

"Because I want to watch your face as I fuck you to it."

There's a protest inside of me, somewhere, that wants to tell him this is the last time. That we don't even like each other. That having sex with my nemesis is the stupidest thing I can do and I don't want it.

But when his teeth nip my ear, I really don't give a shit about any of those reasons.

He takes my arm, placing it up around his neck. "Since the other day, I have thought of you nonstop. I swear, when I saw you downstairs, I thought I was imagining it. But here you are, and now I'm trying to decide what to do with you."

His hand cups my breast, and I rest my head on his chest. How does this man make me feel so good?

I groan when his touch falls away and he steps back. "What happened?" I ask, turning to him.

"Why did you come to my apartment?"

My stomach drops. "For the case," I repeat.

"I don't think so. Tell me why you're here."

The pounding of my heart is loud in my ears and I take a step toward him. Cayden and I do this dance, where one has to surrender. I came here for him. I walked the fifteen minutes here because I was desperate for him—for this.

We're now inches apart and I have to crane my neck to look in his eyes. "Why do you care?"

"Tell me."

Damn him for making me say it.

"Because I want you."

He grins, like the cat that ate the canary and grips my hips. "Do you know where I was going when I was leaving?"

I have a very strong feeling I know, but I want to hear it too. I want for him to lay his cards out on the table so I am not the only one risking it all. "No."

"I think you do."

"If I did, I wouldn't have said no."

He raises one brow. "Considering you lied about why you were here this whole time, I don't believe you."

"Where were you going?" I push back.

"I was coming to find you. To apologize for your office and then beg you to let me make it up to you."

"And how did you plan to do that?"

His hand moves up my back, plastering me to his chest. "It involved my mouth." He kisses me. "My hands." Another kiss. "My tongue." This kiss lasts a little longer as he thrusts it in my mouth. I wrap my arms around his neck, not wanting him to pull away again. I get the point, now I want what was promised.

Cayden leans down, gripping my thighs and lifting me. The music plays and I hear the steady thrum of the bass. It pulses around us, as he moves into his room.

"This bed is going to be ruined for me," he says, before kissing me deeper.

All of the questions I have are gone, all that lives in this space is him. I really wish he wasn't so all consuming, it would make this so much easier to walk away.

Although, I don't even know what I'd be walking away from. All we're doing is sex. All we can be is sex.

It's easy to screw someone you hate, right?

I have to hate him. I have to hold onto that anger because it fuels me to be a better lawyer.

He breaks away from my mouth just long enough to pull my top off, free my breasts and then kiss his way down. Gone is the smooth, in-control man I know well. He's like an animal freed. He sucks my nipple into his mouth and moves his hand to my shorts.

"I want them off. I want you naked," his voice is ragged.

I move to do just that, wanting the same from him, and as I pull mine off, Cayden strips down. When we're both completely naked, he climbs over me, but I want something first.

I need it.

"Lie on your back." I take charge, deciding, again, this is the last time. I better make it count.

He does, putting his hands behind his head. "What now?"

I slide my finger down his chest slowly, watching his abs flex as I reach the beginning of his stomach. "Now you have to suffer for a little."

"Suffer?"

I nod. "Well, it won't really be painful, but you have to stay just like that. It's my turn to explore."

"Explore away."

I move lower, just touching the tip of his cock, which already has precum leaking from it. I do this to him. I make him just as crazy as he does to me. I pull my hair to the side, so he can see my face as I move to where my hand is.

"Hadley," he groans my name.

"Keep your hands there," I remind him. "Don't move."

I see his arms tense and I am going to enjoy every second of his agony. Each time we've done this, he's been in control, it's going to be nice to have the tables turned.

My lips brush his cock and he moans. Then, without wanting to drag this out, I take him deep in my mouth, sucking hard. The beat of the music spurs me on and I keep time, just as he wished to do. At some point I lose focus on staying in time and let his noises be the new music.

"Hadley, baby, you have to stop!" He calls out.

I don't pay attention, I want him to lose control. I want him to know how it feels to be at someone's mercy the way he's done to me.

Taking him deeper, I work to relax my throat even more and then, before I can even gasp, I'm on my back and Cayden is on top.

He doesn't say anything, he doesn't have to as his eyes are wild. There is no mistaking who is in charge again. I may have gotten that sliver of time, but it's over now.

Cayden lifts my legs to rest on his shoulders and then surges forward, filling me so quickly it robs my breath.

The two of us are frantic, both reaching for each other as he thrusts deeper. I want to say something to him, but there are no coherent words inside of me.

All that exists is us.

The pace he sets has me at the edge of my orgasm in seconds. I scream his name as I fall over moments later. Then he calls out my name and we be both melt into the bed.

* * * *

"What time to do you have to be at work?" Cayden asks as his finger makes patterns on my back.

I smile, tucking the pillow under my head so I can look at him. "Soon. I have to go home, shower, and change. I'm not going back to work in what I wore yesterday."

"The ultimate walk of shame?"

"No shame."

We had sex two more times last night and then once this morning. I didn't know it was humanly possible to have that many orgasms in twelve hours, but here we are.

"No, no shame in what we're doing."

"But we can't keep doing this, Cayden."

His hand stops for just a moment and then begins again. "So, this is the last time?"

"I think we both know it should be."

"But it doesn't have to be."

I sigh, and roll away from him, tucking the sheet under my arms. "It has to be."

"Why?"

"Because we can't just keep having sex when we're opposing counsel on a case. It's so unprofessional it's not even funny"

He shakes his head. "No one has to know what we do when we're not at work. There was nothing about the case or anything other than the two of us."

Maybe that's true, but it's still wrong. "And when someone finds out?"

"We're adults and what we do is our business."

I sit up, knowing this argument is going to be like every other. Neither of us ever gives in. I can't just keep screwing him and pretending as though I don't have feelings for him. My heart will get mangled by the end of this.

"Hadley, get back in bed," Cayden urges.

If I do, I'll end up being talked into some agreement that I know is a mistake. I've already made enough of those where he's concerned.

"I have to go to work."

"You mean you have to run away."

I pull my shirt on, then my pants before addressing him. I need whatever armor I can gather. "You can call it what you want. You can put forth your argument just the same as I have. The bottom line is, in the end, someone will get hurt, and let's be honest, it'll be me. I have a career I'm building and I refuse to let you derail it."

"Who said I want to derail it?"

"No one, but that's how it goes, and I would rather walk away now without any complications."

Which isn't true, I'm already emotionally involved.

"If that's what you want," Cayden says, throwing his legs over the side of the bed, clearly pissed.

It's not what I want, but look how easily and quickly he gave in. Not even an attempt to fight harder. And if there's one thing Cayden is really good at, it's arguing his point. That's not happening here.

So, I straighten my spine as he sits with his back to me and fortify the walls around my heart so I can walk out of here.

"Goodbye, Cayden."

"Bye."

All right then.

I walk out of the room, head held high, and make my way down the elevator, to the street, and away from him, with tears streaming down my face each step of the way.

I'm such a fool.

Chapter Twelve

CAYDEN

God she's beautiful.

Seven days have done nothing to diminish my feelings. I've tried—and failed. Hadley is under my skin and I am either going to win her or I have to leave this city. I can't live in this limbo and the fact that I am this fucked in the head over her seems insane.

But it's how I feel.

For seven days I have done nothing other than think of her. I lay on the pillow she slept on, clinging to the disappearing scent.

She walked out and while it fucking killed me to let her go, I'm aware the only way to win her over, is to show her. I have poured myself into doing anything that doesn't remind me of her.

Except, somehow, I have found a way to conjure her into that moment. Not even going to Logan's game got me out of it and I love baseball.

It didn't help that they were playing the Red Sox so I wondered the entire time if Hadley was happy when they scored a run or if she was sad at the end when they lost.

This is the pathetic man I have become.

"Do your clients agree, Mr. Hennington?" Hadley asks, her eyes fixed on mine.

"I'm sorry, what was it you proposed?" Great. Now I look like a damn idiot in front of my colleague and hers.

She sighs. "I offered that you would increase the money by sixteen million dollars and my clients are willing to remove one of the requested seats. It would allow them to still have a voice in the plans as well as compensate them for the removal of the majority seat holdings."

It's absolutely more money than it's worth. That seat is not worth sixteen million dollars. I laugh once. "I see you are working on some interesting valuations. Where exactly did that number come from? It's more than double the purchase price of the property."

She raises one shoulder. "Yes, but as the contract is written now, my clients get the six million dollars as well as two seats. So, in order to make up for the loss of the seat, they need to be compensated fairly."

"I'm not denying that, but this isn't a charity either, Ms. Arrowood. This is a piece of land—that is in decay, I might add. It's not worth twenty-two million dollars."

"We never implied it is. We are stating the land's value remains at the agreed purchase price. We're discussing the seat on the board so they don't turn it into a strip mall."

That's exactly what Mike is going to do. "My client would be well within his rights to do whatever he wants as he'll hold the deed."

Hadley grins. "But at this time, he doesn't. In fact, we can walk out of here right now and sue you for breach of contract because as it's written, they get six million dollars and two seats on the board, which is what you're here trying to rectify, are you not?"

I'd like to rectify the fact that I want to strip you down and make you come on my tongue.

I shake my head, forcing that particular vision away. "Then they can have the two seats."

I'm not sure if this is going to work, but I need to push her.

"I see. You no longer wish to negotiate?" Hadley asks.

I stand, grabbing the papers, putting them in a neat pile, and, using the oldest negotiation tactic known to man, decide to walk out. "I would, if that's what we were doing here, but you're asking for more than double the cost of the land, which is not within my client's best interests to pay. This was a simple transaction and now it's extortion."

Hadley laughs softly. "Sit down, Cayden."

I lift my gaze to hers and she's sitting back, legs crossed, swaying back and forth in her seat. And I want to fall to my knees in front of her.

"We're done here."

"We're not. Sit down. You're not going to walk away. You could at least counteroffer, but you're too stubborn to lose so you're bluffing to walk out."

I stop moving, watching her in complete ease. "No, I'm walking out. There's no bluff."

It's a bluff, but I'm committed now.

"Fine." She smiles at me and gets to her feet. "Thank you for coming. I'll let my clients know that the contract stands as it was written."

Fuck. She played me.

I have no goddamn upper hand. Mike was crystal clear, he wants that seat back. He definitely didn't say pay another sixteen million though. And Hadley knows me well enough that I wouldn't agree to it. She also knows that my competitive nature wouldn't let her push this meeting, which is why she began out of the gate aggressively.

I was blinded and now I have to fix it. Because the bottom line is that my clients want that seat.

I turn to her, hands resting on the table. "You need to do better if you want more money."

She rises like a warrior, mimicking my stance. "You need that seat back and you're going to have to pay for it." Then she pushes upright, standing tall. "I'll await your call with a counter offer. Oh, and Cayden?"

"Yes?"

"It better knock their socks off."

* * * *

A week later we are sitting in the board room, our clients as well, since I am not willing to do this back-and-forth thing. I am on a ticking time bomb and need to fix this stupid case today.

"Do you have an offer for my client?" Hadley asks. Her long brown hair is down today. She normally has it pulled back in a tight bun when she's at work. When I saw her, I was momentarily rendered speechless.

Although that seems to be a norm with us.

"Yes, we have a counter offer that we believe you'll all be happy with."

Our last meeting was seven days ago. I went to my clients, who were really unhappy about having to shell out more money, and Mike's counteroffer was a joke. There was not a chance in hell Hadley's clients would ever take it, but my job is to at least bring it to the table and see. When I called Hadley, she laughed and hung up, not even saying a word.

I explained, once again, to Mike that he was going to have to bend a lot more, to which we went back and forth on an offer that I think she'll actually entertain.

"Please, let's hear it."

"My client is prepared to allow you to keep the one seat on the board, but also provide you with two things." I slide the contract addendum to them. "First, is the lump sum of six million dollars, which is clearly much lower than the twenty you asked for, but please allow me to give you the second portion of the deal." Hadley's eyes narrow and then widen as she reads it. "As much as it seems this is about money, land, and seats on the board, I believe it's about much more to you—legacy. It's about the land your grandfather had, and his grandfather before that. You don't actually want the seats on the board, or maybe you do, but my client is a developer. However, his desires for this land are not what you assume and he is willing to contractually agree that he will not build or tear anything down without your approval."

Her client gasps and then looks to Mike. "I don't understand. Why would you do that? Why would you buy it if your entire goal wasn't to develop on it?"

Mike looks to me and I nod. I was very clear he wasn't allowed to talk because he's a freaking hothead and we needed to keep it calm, but I actually think it's important he says this part. "When we bought the property, it wasn't because we wanted to put a parking lot there. I bought it because the land that butts the property was my grandfather's. I have been waiting to buy something close to where he grew up for years. Yes, I plan to build a smaller sized resort, but not right away. I may never do it."

"You don't want to put up a mall or something else?" Her clients ask in confusion.

"No. If we did build on there, to start it would be a house so my father can live there, where my grandfather is buried."

Which is why he wanted this done so quickly that he agreed to terms he never should've.

Hadley's eyes meet mine and understanding swims there. She leans in to her clients, whispering in their ears. They nod and say something back so I do the same to Mike.

"I think they'll take it."

"I hope so. My father doesn't have much time."

It took a two-hour conversation to finally get to the heart of why he wanted the deed so fast, but also was hesitant on just telling me the truth. He needed to say the land was a business investment so that he could buy it through his company. The board could've vetoed the sale if they thought it was never going to be developed.

So, this is the compromise we came up with that hopefully helps everyone.

Hadley clears her throat. "My clients accept these terms."

The paperwork is signed, everyone is happy—except for me. Because I don't know when I'll see her again, and I can't handle that thought.

Chapter Thirteen

HADLEY

Oh, God. No. No, no, no, no. I look at the pregnancy test results again. I cannot be freaking pregnant.

I am on the pill.

I'm also stupid because I've missed a day and have been having massive amounts of unprotected sex.

Melanie knocks on the bathroom stall door in my office building. "Had? What are the results?"

I called my cousin after I threw up again before my meeting with Cayden. I thought it could be nerves, but then it happened again just after I walked past an intern who was having a tuna sandwich.

After that I did some mental math and realized I'm two weeks late. I am never late.

"It's wrong," I tell her.

"Wrong because it's negative?" The hope in her voice is cute.

I push the door open, tears running down my cheeks and I hand her the test. She doesn't need to look at it to know what the results are though.

"Oh, shit."

"Yeah."

"You're pregnant," Melanie confirms what I already know.

"I am pregnant with Cayden's baby." I laugh because I'm already crying. "I mean, sure, why not? It's like the worst possible scenario that could ever play out."

"Not the worst, but...not the point."

I wipe my cheeks and blow my nose. "What am I going to do?"

"What do you want to do?" Mel asks. "You have options..."

I don't really. I mean, I do, but this isn't just some random guy in a bar. Or a man who has ever disrespected me. It's Cayden…the man I am stupidly in love with.

"I have to talk to him before I decide anything."

She pulls me into her arms and I let her love and support surround me. "I know, right now, it doesn't feel like it, but this will be okay. You are strong and smart. You have an amazing job."

I sniff as the tears fall. "I am unmarried and we all know how the family feels about that."

Melanie pulls back and purses her lips. "Yeah, but, screw them. They aren't the pillars of perfect living. They love you, Hadley. They love all of us beyond the point of normal, but they care. I know we're all off our rockers, but there's nothing we wouldn't do for each other. You know that."

"I definitely do. God, my dad."

Melanie tries to hold back her laugh, but it escapes anyway. "Now, Cayden may not have any options because he's going to be dead."

"I have to tell him."

"Who? Your dad?" Mel asks, her eyes wide.

"No, not my dad. I mean, sure I'll have to tell him too, but not now. Jesus, maybe once I'm actually giving birth you can call him and let him know."

She laughs at that. "Yeah, so not going to do that. If anyone is telling him, we'll make it be Bethanne. He's less likely to kill her."

I snort. "He'd put her in a convent for fear she'd be next."

Mel smiles and then rubs my back. "You don't have to tell Cayden right away. Give yourself a few days to come to terms with it. Figure out what you want first, then you guys can discuss it. Maybe see the doctor too. Confirm that what this test says is right. It could be a false positive."

That sliver of hope hangs out there. Maybe she's right.

"I'll call today."

"Good, and I love you and…we'll be like two women and a baby. It'll be fun. I'll make them clothes and Auntie Mel will be the best."

Yeah, I can't even go there. Not now. Not until I know for sure.

* * * *

"I'm pregnant," I say to my sister over the phone. This morning, I had my first appointment at my OBGYN and sure enough, I am with child.

Bethanne goes silent.

"Beth?"

"You are…pregnant?"

"Yup. And no one knows other than Mel. So please keep your mouth shut. I don't want to tell anyone yet."

I can imagine my sister's face right now. "Are you happy?"

What a loaded question. It's hard to explain what I am because it changes every damn minute. In thirty seconds I can go from one extreme to another. "I don't know if I'd say that I'm happy, but I am not unhappy. If that makes any sense."

"It does," Beth says with understanding only a sister can have. "And you haven't told anyone?"

"No. I don't know when I will, but for now, I want to just keep this a secret. We just…don't have secrets."

Beth laughs. "Umm, other than the fact you've been banging someone and got pregnant."

Yeah, that part I left out. "It's complicated."

"I'm sure it is. Does the father know?"

My sister knows about Cayden and for some reason, I'm not ready to tell her that it's him. I want to tell him before I tell anyone else. He has a right to know he's the father before my sister does.

"Not yet. I have to tell him. I just wanted to make sure with the doctor first."

"Okay, I'm not going to ask who, because you seem reluctant to tell me, but…do you at least like the guy?"

I smile, thinking of Cayden. "I do. A lot."

"Oh, thank God. I thought maybe you had a lapse in judgment and slept with that guy from college again."

Yeah, that's exactly what happened.

"I will probably wait to tell everyone until I'm home at Christmas. It's better to get the whole family out of the way at once."

Beth gasps. "You want me to keep this a secret for *months*? Are you crazy? I have to go home for freaking Thanksgiving. I'm supposed to just lie to Mom? Is that even possible? That woman is like a human lie detector with us. Ugh! Hadley!"

I cringe because she's right, I am asking her to lie to Mom, which is so damn hard to do. "Just…avoid answering. Pretend I never told you."

"Right. I'll do that." Someone calls my sister's name in the background and she sighs. "I have to go. We have practice in five minutes and you know I'm always late so they've sent a crew to collect me now."

I smile. "Okay. I love you."

"Love you too. I really do and I'll keep your secret. You know that."

"I do. The doctor warned things can happen in the beginning so it's better we don't say anything."

"All right. I'll call you in a few days," Beth promises, which we both know she won't.

"Okay."

She hangs up and I lie back in my bed, wondering how I am going to tell the next and most important person—Cayden.

Chapter Fourteen

CAYDEN

I'm leaning against her building, waiting for her to exit. I know she hasn't yet, because my office called up to hers to see if we could have a meeting tomorrow and she answered, accepting the offer.

So, I'm here, stalking her, like a psycho.

Twenty minutes later, she emerges. I move to her with my iced coffee and she stops. "Cayden? We have a meeting tomorrow. Why are you here?"

I grin as her lips turn into a smile. "I need us to keep the peace. We've had a rocky road as of late."

Hadley sighs. "Yeah, but I was prepared to see you tomorrow. I have to go. I can't talk today. I'm not ready." She starts to walk away.

I'm not sure what she's supposed to be ready for. All I asked for was a meeting. Which was really just a ploy to see her again. I would've made some bullshit up, but when the idea of seeing her again tomorrow became possible, I couldn't wait.

"Dinner."

"What?"

Here goes my Hail Mary. "Have dinner with me."

"Why?"

"Because I want to take you out to dinner. You have to eat, don't you? I think we can manage to share a meal?"

"But...we have a meeting tomorrow."

"Yes, but I'm hungry and I'd like to just talk."

Her pause gives me hope. "One meal. No sex."

Victory is mine.

"I will do my best to keep you from mauling me."

"Yeah, I'm sure that'll be the issue," she says with a smile. "So, where are you taking me?"

"Come on, let's find out."

We head to the subway and go a few stops toward the theater district. "You're taking me to a show?"

"I said dinner, but if I was planning a show, it would be *Wicked*."

"Oh, because you identify with Elphaba?" she asks.

"I am totally the good witch here."

Hadley snorts. "Please. Did you know my cousin is on Broadway?"

"What?"

She nods. "Sebastian, Melanie's brother. He has a pretty big role and, not to sound biased, but he's amazing and has always had a flare for the dramatics."

"A family trait considering your uncle is a big Hollywood star. Must be hard growing up in the Arrowood family, with everyone around you always in the spotlight."

Her whole family is pretty fucking amazing. Her dad was a Navy SEAL, Declan is some mogul in business, Sean just retired from being a major league star who hit a walk off in the World Series, and then Jacob Arrowood is…well, Jacob Arrowood.

Hadley grins before bumping my arm with her shoulder. "It has its challenges. Our family worked really hard to protect us though. We spent a lot of time on the farm to avoid the spotlight. It's crazy because we're all pretty grounded. Deep family values with strict parents."

I laugh at that one. "I know it all too well. My parents weren't really strict, they just have very high expectations of us. I never wanted to disappoint my mom, she'd been through hell after my dad's suicide."

I don't talk about it a lot. There's really not much to say, but I want to be open with Hadley. I want her to see this isn't just some fuckfest, I want more.

"I remember you mentioned it."

I nod. "I was ten. I remember everything from that day. My mother's face, the lights outside my house, and then learning he was dead. I didn't know how he died, just that he was gone. Mom protected us from the truth for a long time."

"I'm so sorry, Cayden," Hadley takes my hand in hers and I wrap my fingers around it, not wanting to let go.

She looks at our joined hands as we walk down 44th Street. I talk so she doesn't try to remove hers. "We all survived. I'm more upset at all the things he missed. He loved watching Logan play ball, and he'll never see him in front of thousands of Yankee fans screaming his name. He'll never see us get married or have kids. I was angry for a really long time. Now, I'm more sad than anything."

"It's difficult to forgive, I'm sure."

I nod. "You understand that."

I know about Hadley's past as well. During a lecture on protective orders and the issues the legal system needs reformed most, Hadley became very, very angry. She and our professor went toe-to-toe until she finally screamed that unless he'd been a little girl screaming as she ran to get help as her mother was being beaten within an inch of her life, he could keep his opinion to himself.

"I do. Kevin, my mother's ex-husband who I thought was my father for years, did things that I can't really ever understand. I'm...lucky though. My mother was brave and my real dad found us. However, Daddy is incredibly protective of his girls. Bethanne and I never discussed boys around him. It was better for everyone."

"So, I should be worried when we meet?"

Her eyes fill with a million questions. "Are you thinking you're going to meet my dad?"

"Once you finally admit you're in love with me, it's going to happen."

Hadley laughs. "In love with you? I think you're a bit ahead of yourself there, buddy."

Not a denial. "Allow me to rephrase. Are you in love with me?" I ask, standing outside of the restaurant my client owns, where he's set up a table in a cozy nook where we can finally talk.

Her mouth parts, closes, and then opens again. "I...don't...we have to talk."

"I thought so."

I open the door and wave her inside where we head to our table. We order a bottle of wine, and the waiter lets me know the chef has already prepared our menu. Hadley asks for her wine glass to have soda instead.

She looks around and pulls her lower lip between her teeth. "How in the world did you ever find this place?"

"The owner is a client of mine. He also happens to have the best Italian food in New York."

"I'm a happy girl."

"Good. I'm also going to pretend it's not because of the food, but because of the company you're with."

"Pretend away." She pulls the glass to her lips, taking a small sip, but I see the smile behind it.

"I know our meeting is tomorrow, but I wanted to discuss it beforehand."

"So, this isn't a date?"

"It's a date," I clarify.

"With career intentions behind it."

I shake my head. "No, I never should've said it, but…" I reach out, pulling her hand to mine, and laying the other on top. "I'm on shaky ground here, Hadley. I have spent the last two weeks doing everything I can to get you out of my head and instead, you've taken up residence. If I'm honest, it's been like this since college."

"You terrify me, Cayden."

"Why?" She tries to pull her hand back, but I don't want her to do that. "Don't pull away."

"If I don't, you're going to hate me."

"Why do you say that?"

"Because I won't be able to stop myself from falling so hard, so incredibly hard that I will never be able to get up again."

I move closer, needing her to hear this, knowing there may never be another chance to tell her how I feel. Hadley has trust issues, I know all too well, and I haven't exactly given her a reason to trust me. I want that chance though, and I am going to lay it all out now and hope like hell she doesn't run away. "I'll lift you up. I'll carry you if your legs won't work. I'll hold you together if you are falling apart. You may be worried about falling, Hadley Arrowood, but I'm already there. I'm on the ground, asking you to sit with me because I think we could be something pretty damn amazing. Give me a chance to show you how much you mean to me already."

Hadley's eyes are brimming with tears. "I'm pregnant."

Chapter Fifteen

HADLEY

Well, subtlety was never my strong suit and I couldn't let him keep saying these amazing things without knowing the truth.

It has been hard enough, with his lingering touches over dinner, to have not blurt it out until now.

I couldn't hold back. I couldn't keep it in any longer.

I'm pregnant and…he has to know.

"You're pregnant?" he asks.

"I found out a few days ago. I went to the doctor and it's confirmed. I'm only about six weeks."

Cayden leans back, probably doing the math in his head. "So, the first time?"

"Yeah, or the second, they weren't exactly weeks apart."

"Wow," he says, pushing his dark hair back, which is his tell for the fact that he's piecing things together.

"I'm not asking for anything, Cayden. I'm going to keep the baby, and I don't want you to feel obligated. You don't have to be involved or help financially. I can handle it all."

He moves so quickly, I almost jump. "I don't feel obligation to you or the baby."

"Well, okay then." I know I said I didn't want him to, but that was a little too easy of a statement.

"I didn't mean it that way. I'm sorry. Of course I feel obligated. Jesus, I can't get this right. Okay, let me start again. This wasn't where I thought tonight would go, but it's here. You're here and now we're having a baby. I…am shocked, but also, I don't know, happy?"

I smile a little and hope starts to form. After all he said, I prayed that maybe we could be together. I wouldn't require it because that's not who I am, but I want it. I want him and us and the baby to have this chance at love and happiness.

"What about all you said before?"

His hands cup mine, holding them so tenderly. "I meant it all. I think I fell in love with you the day we met and you told me I was a pompous asshole."

"You were."

He laughs. "I was, but you smiled at me and I was gone. Then we had that night and I fucked up afterwards, trying to brush it off like it meant nothing."

I try not to think about it because it hurts. Cayden was only the second person I'd ever slept with. I was very careful who I let into my heart. After witnessing my mother make the wrong choice with a man right out of college, I was terrified to repeat the mistakes of her past.

Cayden seemed so different. He was nice, when he wasn't a know-it-all. Even then, there wasn't malicious intent. The day I fought with my professor about domestic violence, it was Cayden who spoke up in my defense, when normally, he was battling against me.

"We were really young and stupid."

"My point is that we're not now. I'm not scared and I'm not going to walk away. I want to be with you, Hadley. I want to come over after work, sit on the floor, eat pizza, and bitch about my day. I want to fall asleep with you in my arms and wake up and you be the first thing I see. We have a lot of crap to figure out, but I'm here because there's nowhere else I'd rather be."

"So, you want to date me?" I ask, feeling a little strange even saying the words.

"Yes."

"You're sure? Because I can be a single mother. I can...raise this baby and do all the things if you don't want that. Dating me means that you're also accepting our child."

"Do you listen at all, woman?" Cayden huffs. "I love you. I know that sounds insane, but I love you."

I pull my hands away and cup his face. "I love you, too."

He brings his lips to mine and it's the softest, sweetest kiss I've ever shared with another person.

I can feel all the emotions and all of this is crazy, but yet so perfect.

The waiter clears his throat and we break apart, heat filling my cheeks. "Sorry."

He smiles, placing the first course in front of us. "It is nice to see two people in love."

Cayden and I eat the soup, it's absolutely amazing. Today was a good day with my stomach, I have been able to keep everything down. Yesterday was a different story.

"What did the doctor say?" Cayden asks after our plates are cleared.

"Not much. I go back in a few weeks, and I'll monitor everything. I'm not ready to tell anyone yet."

"Why?"

"I don't want anyone at work to know. I've seen what happens to a woman's career once they say they're starting a family. The partners at my firm are great, but I would like to continue proving myself before I say anything. As for everyone else, we're really early into this pregnancy. Things can happen, and...I don't want to tell people we're pregnant to then tell people we're not pregnant."

Cayden nods. "I respect that. I'm assuming Melanie knows?"

"Yes," I say with a soft laugh. "She brought me the test and was there when I took it. My sister, Bethanne, also knows. She doesn't know you're the father, but just that I'm pregnant. I am not really sure why I told her, other than I had gotten home from the doctor and needed to talk to someone..."

"You could've called me," he suggests.

I could've. Maybe even should've. I just wasn't really ready to do that. It was too real to talk to Cayden about the child we created. I never thought he would flip or be unsupportive, not that I thought we'd end up being together at the end, but I just needed to sit with it.

"Next time I need to talk, I will."

"I hope so. I really do love you, Hadley. I know it's crazy and it feels like it came out of nowhere."

I stop him there, resting my palm on his face. "It doesn't. I think you're right, we've been falling in love for years. It's just finally come to light. We definitely did all this backwards though."

He laughs. "No shit. But going forward it'll be different."

"How so?"

"Well, for starters, we're going to go on a real date. One where I ask you, not accost you outside your building."

I nod. "That's a good start."

"Then, we'll go on said date, and you'll be unable to stop touching me."

"Really? Why is that?"

"Because I'm charming and handsome."

I lean back in my chair with a smile. "Is that so?"

"Clearly, you're already in love with me."

"This is true. I also am pregnant with your baby, so it totally could be that."

Cayden shakes his head as though it's not even possibly the reason. "It's my charm."

"I'm so glad you are able to tell the difference."

"Considering you are the first and only woman to have or be carrying my child, and others have also found me to be rather irresistible, we can draw a very clear conclusion that it is, in fact, me."

I raise one brow, fighting back the urge to giggle like a freaking school girl. "I feel that your argument lacks substance and is leading. You haven't disproved the evidence of the hormones and pheromones being present during this encounter. Professor Stein would be very displeased with your argument."

"He liked you better anyway"

"This is true."

Our next course is served and the conversation turns to more lighthearted things. He wants me to come to a game with him next week and meet his brother. As much as I hate admitting that this excites me, it does. His brother is freaking amazing, even my Uncle Sean thinks it.

"I'm totally going to be nervous," I admit between bites.

"Meeting Logan?"

"Yeah, he's…well, he's Logan Benson-Hennington."

"And your uncle is Sean Arrowood. Forget even him, your other uncle is freaking Jacob Arrowood."

"Yeah, but they're not as cool as people think."

He puts both hands out in front of him with that face like…duh. "My point."

"But Logan isn't my uncle. He's your brother."

"Which makes him even less cool." Cayden's hand rests on my leg. "Listen, Logan will love you. He is the one person that I would like to tell about the baby. I know we said we wouldn't but I wouldn't doubt if I have two missed calls from him now."

"Why?"

He sighs. "Because he's annoying and nosey. He knew I was coming on a date, he knows how I feel about you, and we tell each other pretty much everything. Plus there's this weird twin thing."

I can understand that. "Then we should tell him. I am just trying to avoid many people knowing until we're out of the danger zone and then I think I am going to wait until the baby is born to tell my family." As much as I'm kidding, I'm not.

My dad is going to lose his shit.

Cayden laughs. "Yeah, my parents aren't going to take it well."

"Tell me about it." He leans in, pressing his lips to mine. "We have time, and until then, I'll spoil you, make you love me even more than you do now, and we'll keep the baby a secret."

I wrap my arms around his neck, not caring that we're in public and kiss him a little harder. "I look forward to the spoiling part."

"You should. Are you still hungry?"

We haven't had the main course, but I'm pretty full. "Not really."

He lifts his hand, waving the waiter over. "Check please."

"What?" I ask.

"I'm hungry, but not for food. My apartment is six blocks from here and I'd much rather eat something else."

This spoiling thing is going to be really fun.

Chapter Sixteen

CAYDEN

~Four months later~

"Where did you put the box with the dishes?" Hadley yells from the second bedroom, where all of my things are still being sorted.

"Probably in the kitchen."

Moving in together has been challenging. Melanie, unbeknownst to Hadley, has been dating her boss and things have progressed to the point they are discussing marriage. Their lease was coming up and she asked if Hadley would be upset if she moved out, which would give Hadley two bedrooms for her and the baby.

I don't know what exactly came over me but the idea of her living alone while she's pregnant was too much. I suggested we move in together, presenting a compelling argument that she couldn't refuse.

It's been two weeks and I think she's ready to kill me.

She comes out of the bedroom, hair on top of her head, and a scowl on her face. "You have to unpack. We can't live like this. I am seriously losing my mind in this chaos."

"I know."

"You know or you're going to fix it?"

The laughter from the living room causes both our eyes to turn. "Shut up, Logan," I warn.

"I'm not saying anything, just that Hadley is right and you're a mess."

She smiles at my brother. "Thank you and you are very quickly becoming my favorite Hennington."

Logan beams. "See, I told you that you're lacking."

"You're going to be lacking some teeth if you keep it up."

He shrugs. "Hadley will protect me."

She rolls her eyes and then turns to me. "We have to donate some of this, babe. We don't need all these things. Melanie took a lot, but we've already figured those housewares out. Please, I want to start preparing the room for the baby."

I move to her, wrapping my arms around her, pulling her to me. When she's in my arms, it's like all the world is settled. I kiss her forehead, keeping my lips there an extra second. "I'll take care of it this weekend. We can go through the boxes, get rid of what we don't need so we can get the nursery together."

"Thank you," she squeezes and rests her head on my chest.

"You know I'd do anything for you."

She looks up. "Except get rid of that ugly statue."

Logan and I both laugh. My mom and Aunt Angie went through this phase where they suddenly thought they had untapped art potential. They took a sculpting class in Nashville, where they came home with the most ridiculous pieces of what they called art. Dad warned Logan and I that we better not say anything disrespectful or he'd have us mucking the stalls for a year.

Being the assholes we are, the two of us gushed over it. I mean over the top ridiculous praise.

My father convinced her that since we loved it so much, we needed to take it with us wherever we lived. So, we had a piece of her with us.

I look at Logan. "It's your turn to take it."

"Hell no it isn't. I get it almost all season so no one has to look at it. It's November now, buddy. I am going to enjoy the hell out of not seeing it until Spring season starts."

Hadley's eyes narrow on him. "I am having a baby, Logan. I am... I am emotional and it causes me to feel sad and I can't..." The tears start and I am impressed.

Logan gets to his feet quickly. "Hadley, don't cry."

"I can't look at it without feeling so many things," the fake tears are coming harder now. She sniffs. "I just...please...you have to take it."

Logan is nodding before he can speak. "Of course. I'll take it. Don't cry, Jesus, it's not worth getting upset over. Cayden, make her stop."

She wipes her eyes. "You mean it? You'll take it?"

"Yes, I'll call a few of the guys and we'll get it out of here tonight. I promise."

She exhales, smiles wide, and then hugs him. "Thanks!"

"You...you played me!"

"I did. Thank you! Happy Thanksgiving!" She lifts her hand and saunters into the kitchen.

"That woman is trouble," he says and I stand here, staring in the direction she went.

"That woman is going to be my wife someday."

* * * *

"That one," I tell the jeweler. "That's the one."

I spent the last four hours staring at different kinds of engagement rings with her cousin helping.

"She's going to love it," Melanie assures me.

"I think so too."

"When are you going to pop the question?"

I wanted to do it before we went home for Christmas, but I haven't figured out if I'll do it at her house or mine.

"Probably depends if her dad kills you at her house."

Yeah, there's that part.

"Well, if I survive next week, I guess we'll find out then."

"I'm really happy for you guys."

"Have you told your parents that you're living with your boss yet?" I ask after handing over my credit card.

"No, we aren't like you guys. We are having a lot of fun, living together is great, but I don't know that I want to marry him. And after his nasty divorce three years ago, I'm not sure he wants it either. For now, this works for us." She smiles widely. "Plus, if I did, then the attention wouldn't be on you for the Arrowood Christmas Extravaganza."

She is having way too much fun with this. Hadley has a big case that she's currently working on. Her boss wants it signed before the holidays, so we may not get on the road until late Christmas Eve.

"You know that you guys have me fucking terrified."

Melanie rests her hand on my shoulder. "Cayden, you should be. I'm not trying to make it sound worse than it will be. I'm giving you my honest opinion. The Arrrowood brothers are not normal. They love their children and…they're nuts. Good luck."

I grab the bag from the cashier, feeling nauseous after basically paying for what feels like a down payment on a house. "Well, I love her. She's worth it."

"Lead with that, my friend."

Mel heads off to do whatever Mel does and I have a missed call from my mother.

I dial it back, and start the walk back to my office where I can keep the ring away from Hadley.

"Cayden! Hi, sweetheart."

"Hi, Mom."

"How is work?"

"Work is good, is that what you called for?"

She scoffs. "No, I called because it's been almost two weeks since I've heard from you and I wanted to make sure no one murdered you."

I laugh. "I'm alive."

"Clearly. You know, Logan calls home at least once a week."

"Logan is the better son, what can I say? Some of us have to work for a living."

I can picture my mother's face. "Whatever that means. Are you still coming for Christmas?"

"Yes, but I will be there late Christmas night."

"And you're bringing your girlfriend still?" I can hear how hard she's trying to keep this conversation light, but also it's killing her not to know more about Hadley.

"Yes, I am bringing Hadley. We're going to see her family and then coming to you guys."

"Great. Perfect. I'm so excited to meet her. Logan said she's very beautiful and a lawyer too. He said you like her a lot."

Seems my brother has said a lot. Asshole. "Yes, all of those things are true."

"You like her?"

I sigh. "Mom, I love you."

"I love you too, but you could give me something here. I'm dyin'."

"If I didn't love her, I wouldn't be bringing her home for Christmas."

She gasps. "You love her?"

"I really do."

"Oh... Oh..."

My father's voice comes on the line a second later. "What did you do to make your Mama cry?"

"I fell in love," I admit.

"Well, that'll do it. Can't wait to meet her, Cay. If you're bringin' her home to your Mama, she must be special."

I look down at the bag in my hand with a diamond I plan to put on her finger. "Yeah, Dad, she really is."

Chapter Seventeen

HADLEY

I exhale deeply for the fifth time as we approach Arrowood Farms. Cayden takes my hand, squeezing as we turn to see the wooden frame at the entrance above our long driveway. "I have to stop here why?"

"What's one truth about an arrow?" I ask the sign. Imagining my father's smile as he did to me what my grandmother did to him.

I wonder about her often, if she's happy in heaven watching her sons all grown and living lives she would be proud of.

Though I never met her, she is very much a part of our family.

"Hadley?"

I glance at Cayden. "My grandmother was steeped in traditions. She didn't have an easy life, my grandfather was abusive and…he caused a lot of havoc in the lives of the people I love. My grandmother, according to my father and uncles, was a saint. She walked on water and loved her boys more than anything in this world. Whenever they would pull up to the farm, she would stop at this sign and ask them each the same question…what's one truth about an arrow?"

"I can imagine as ten-year-old boys they loved that."

I giggle. "Oh, they did. Daddy says that he would roll his eyes, and Uncle Declan was the worst. He would try to just stay silent and see if she would give up, but she never did."

"I see where you get it from…"

I slap his chest playfully. "Anyway, the crazy part is that she knew her kids so well, she imparted wisdom in this truth that would help them overcome their own worst fears. So, all of us have them too and while we have never—not once—been forced to stop and say it, none of us will ever let them drive without doing it."

Cayden chuckles. "That's some reverse psychology right there."

I shrug. "Maybe in the beginning, but for me, it feels like I get to know my grandma each time I say it."

He leans across the center console to kiss me. "What's one truth about an arrow?"

"The target might move, but if you move with it, and take the shot at the right time, you'll never miss."

"I like that," he says softly.

"It's funny how true it is. My target never stays stationary and each time I've taken that shot, I've somehow come out okay at the end."

"Like with me."

I smile and shake my head. "Oh, yes, you are the best shot I've ever taken."

"Are you ready to go tell your family? As much as you may want to keep the pregnancy a secret, they're going to see the evidence of it."

In the last two weeks, my once just slightly bloated stomach has very clearly turned into a baby bump. My office has been amazing about not saying anything to my face or asking, but it's clear they're all aware as well. Still, Cayden and I wanted to tell our families before anyone else, even co-workers.

"Let's go."

We arrive at the beautiful house my father had built for my mother. It sits on the back part of the property and the land is divvied up between my uncles. So, we all live fairly close.

"Here goes nothing," I say as we exit.

The front door is unlocked, as it always is, and I push the door open, smiling as my entire family is gathered around in the living room. Dear God, I can't even ease my way into this. All eyes are focused on me, and then shift to Cayden. "Everyone, this is Cayden Benson-Hennington. My boyfriend."

Uncle Sean steps in, reminding us all that he knows a Hennington. "I'm Sean Arrowood, Hadley's uncle and I played ball with your dad. We were good friends and it's been a while since I talked to him, but he met Hadley."

I grip Cayden's arm, hoping it comes across as reassuring. "Yes, I was like, eight and we've covered that." I look at my dad, whose jaw is clenched tight and I can see my mother trying to lend him the same support I am giving Cayden. Might as well get it over with. "Anyway, Cayden, this is my mom and dad."

My mother, who is also a saint, steps forward first. "It's nice to meet you, Cayden. Welcome to our home."

Cayden looks at ease as he moves to her, giving her a hug. "I really appreciate it. We had talked about going to Tennessee and visiting my parents, but Hadley really wanted to come here first. I know it was last minute and a surprise."

Mom gives my dad a stern look. "Well, we're glad you're here, aren't we?"

My father looks like a statue, a very pissed off statue. His brows furrow as he looks at me, probably wishing he could wring my neck since I didn't tell them I was bringing my boyfriend. Then he looks at Cayden. "Yes, welcome. We have guns."

My mother's eyes widen and she tweaks his arm. "Ignore him."

"I was also a SEAL."

"He was also dropped on his head," Mom says.

That's enough. "Daddy!" I really hoped after all this time he could at least pretend to be nice. I was wrong.

"What? I'm letting your boyfriend know that he's in a house with a man who was trained to kill and has firearms. It's like a disclosure agreement. No one can claim they weren't aware of the situation."

Uncle Jacob bursts out laughing and then claps Cayden on the shoulder. "Don't let him scare you, kid. He wasn't a very good or scary SEAL. He worked on phone lines or some shit."

Dad tilts his head with a smirk as he looks at Uncle Jacob. "Want to test that theory?"

"My face is worth millions. I'd like to keep it that way."

The snicker from the room is enough to ease the tension. "Yeah, millions of nothing."

"Let me take your coats." Mom moves forward with her hand outstretched and I panic. Oh, God. No, she can't take my coat. I am not ready for this part. Dad already said he had guns and this is going to go over like a lead balloon. "Hadley?" Mom urges.

I need to do something outside. Yes, where it's cold. Where I can keep my coat on. "Why don't I grab the bags?"

Cayden's hand reaches out. "I'll get them, baby."

This is not a time for chivalry damn it. "I need some air."

And to never have to tell my father what's beneath this coat.

"What's wrong? You're leaving? If it's your father, I'll kill him for you!" My mother promises and then shoots daggers at my father.

God, I am screwing this up so bad. I am a grown woman who is in love with the man beside me. We are having a baby and that's that. I need to stop being a chicken, and face the firing squad…all of them. "Nothing, Mom. It's fine. I'm not leaving. I'm sorry."

"Okay," she says. "Give me your coat and we can get you guys settled upstairs."

"Fine." I remove my coat, watching everyone around me as they see my hand move to my stomach, resting on the bump. "So, Mom, Dad, Cayden and I have some news…"

Dad is the first to speak. "Yes, it's clear you do."

The tone in his voice makes me want to weep. I should've told him sooner, and not like this. He might have been upset, but I miscalculated. Cayden's hand rests on the small of my back, and I take the encouragement he offers. "I wanted to tell you before. I really did, but I've been so busy at the firm and Cayden and I have been trying to get things in order."

Dad looks to Cayden then, ignoring my little tirade. "When's the wedding?"

"Umm, what?"

"The wedding. I expect it's soon? Are you already married?" Dad asks, finally looking at me.

Well, he's out of his damn mind. "Were you married when I was born?" I toss at him.

"Irrelevant. You're pregnant and he needs to marry you."

I look at my family who all seems to think my father is onto something. "Are we in some weird time warp? Since when do we have to get married to have a baby?"

"Since you're my daughter and are pregnant."

Oh, now I'm pissed. Now I want to flip tables. They are all hypocrites and I am going to enjoy this dressing down. My mother grins, as though she knows what's coming from me. I really love my mommy. I take two steps so I'm in front of my father.

"Seriously? What about Bethanne? Were you married when she was conceived? You had two kids without being married." Then, I look at each of my uncles, all of them with children before they were married. "What about you, Uncle Declan? Uncle Sean? Uncle Jacob? Any of you? Are we suddenly to believe that babies out of wedlock aren't a family tradition? I was just keeping the dream alive here, following in all your footsteps."

"She's got us there," Uncle Jacob says. "The girl is too smart for us."

I always loved him. I mean, I love all of them, but Uncle Jacob always spoiled me rotten and he is the most levelheaded about things.

"Shut up, Jacob," Mom says to him. "Hadley, I…I'm just…you're pregnant."

"I am and it's fine. I know it's a bit of a shock and seems fast, but Cayden and I are happy and, well, I hope you'll be too."

Cayden rubs my back, kissing the top of my head. I turn to him, feeling loved and supported. I love him so much and while this was scary, it changes nothing. I am having a baby with him, we have a home, happiness, and nothing will change that. He grins down at me and I know he's thinking the same.

My dad clears his throat and shocks everyone with the words that come out of his mouth. "We're happy if you are."

"We are?" Mom asks.

"She's a grown woman and we've done a good job raising her. Clearly, we missed the safe sex talk somewhere along the way, but…she's always made good choices."

"Thank you, Daddy."

"Congratulations to you both, may you have a daughter so I can sit back and enjoy the hell you're about to endure."

Chapter Eighteen

CAYDEN

Last night I was able to find a few minutes to talk to Hadley's parents alone. I wanted to have the talk and give her father the respect he's owed by informing him of my intentions. It went well, at least I think it did.

I didn't ask for his permission, mostly because it's really not up to him, it's Hadley's choice. However, I did ask for his blessing. Which they both gave.

I roll over, reaching for my future fiancé and she's not there. The sheets are cold and I sit up, looking around for her. I find a note on my side table:

Went to the treehouse to watch the sunrise. I'll be back before you wake, but in case I'm not, I love you.

No idea what treehouse she means, but this gives me a few minutes to get the ring and prepare myself. I'm going to propose today. With the ring in my pocket, I head downstairs. She and her father are sitting by the fireplace, smiling and drinking coffee.

Her eyes light up when she sees me. "Merry Christmas."

I walk over, kissing her nose. "Merry Christmas, sweetheart."

Her mom enters and then her sister comes barreling down the stairs. "Santa came! Oh! My Santa never fails."

Hadley's mother huffs. "Give it up, Beth, you're almost twenty! We know you don't believe."

Beth grins. "You really shouldn't ruin the hopes and dreams of your children, Mother. I know that Santa is real. How else would we have the presents like we do? It's a miracle and each year he reminds me of the miracles that occur."

She and Logan would get along perfectly. Both are smartasses and have that sense of humor that only they understand.

Hadley reaches over into the bag she brought and pulls out a gift, handing it to Beth. "Here, Santa came to my house for you too."

Bethanne grins and takes it. "The spirit of Christmas lives for us believers."

Her mother turns to me while I have my arm thrown around Hadley as her hand sits on her stomach. "I wish I knew you were coming. I hate that you're just sitting here with nothing to open."

"I promise, this is great. I don't need to open anything. I appreciate that I'm not dead or digging my own hole in the field."

Her father laughs. "That can always be arranged."

"It's probably no less than I deserve. I know my mother is going to want to kick my ass when we head there tomorrow."

"The firm doesn't really care about holidays and we're both trying to make partner. Our time is just limited," Hadley explains. "I'm sorry, Mom. I know I've been away, but we'll come out for a weekend soon."

"Now that she doesn't have to hide the pregnancy, she can come back all the time," Beth unhelpfully adds.

Hadley sticks her tongue out and Beth returns the gesture. "Well, I have a present for Cayden. Since I knew he was coming."

"You do?"

"I do."

I like those words from her lips. Not wanting to delay any longer, I get up as well, and grab the bag I had on the side of the couch. "I have something for you too, but I want you to go first."

Hadley unwraps the larger box, to reveal a smaller box inside. "Cayden? What is this?"

My heart is pounding, but as nervous as I am, it's more that I'm just ready. I want this with her and I don't want to wait any longer.

I hear her mother or sister gasp as I take the velvet box from her and drop to my knee. Hadley's eyes fill with tears and I open the lid to show her an emerald cut diamond ring sitting in the center. "I wanted to come here with you so that I could talk to your dad before I did this. I fell in love with you the first time you argued with me in class. You're smart, funny, beautiful, kind, and so much more. I spent two years just trying to get the courage to ask you out and when I did, you said no." They both laugh and she sniffs at the same time. "After our first date, where you spent two hours scolding me about how I was wrong about my stance on a law, I knew there was no other woman for me. Hadley Arrowood, I want to spend the rest of my life loving you and I'm asking you to do me the honor of being my wife?"

She launches herself forward, tears falling and kisses my face. "Yes!"

"Thank God, because it was going to be an awkward ride to Tennessee if you said no."

Her laughter fills the room and her lips find mine again. "How could I say no to you when I have waited my whole life to love someone the way I do you?"

Bethanne squeals and runs to her and they hug and laugh. Connor comes toward me, hand outstretched. "Welcome to the family."

"Thank you."

"Just do right by her and we won't have any issues."

I nod once. "I promise."

Hadley shows her mother the ring and they both cry and hug. Then Ellie makes her way to me. "Oh, I'm so happy. Congratulations! And you're sure you have to leave today?"

"I wish we could stay, but it's a long drive to Bell Buckle and my parents are anxious to meet Hadley."

Her dad laughs. "Who would've thought the man who gave my daughter her horse almost twenty years ago is going to be her father-in-law…you've made her very happy and for that, I thank you."

"There's no thanks needed because she's given me more than I can ever give her."

* * * *

I don't feel half as sick to my stomach as I did going to Hadley's family.

My parents took the news—all of the news—with absolute joy. Mom cried, because that's what she does. My father was worried, but warmed to her immediately, and now I think he likes her better, and my uncles and aunts are already helping pick out baby names.

Hadley reaches over, tapping my shoulder. "Tell them about the time you failed the debate."

"No."

"No, tell them how I was right and you were wrong, it's a great story."

I roll my eyes. "And now she's marrying me."

The ring shimmers in the light and she smiles. "I am. Even though you lost that day."

"One time. One time I was wrong."

"There were more than that, but who's counting?"

Uncle Wyatt chuckles. "Son, you better get used to being wrong. I haven't been right in about fifteen years, right, Angel?"

Aunt Angie sighs. "He wasn't right before that but he had no one to remind him of it."

Hadley grins. "Cayden was right this morning, I'll give him that."

"Last time ever, kid," Dad says.

Logan leans back, tossing his arm behind Hadley. "If he ever does something really dumb, let me know and I'll tell you exactly how to make him hurt."

"And on that note," I say, getting to my feet. "Come on, sweetheart. I want to show you something."

Hadley gets up, and I help her with her coat, wrap a scarf around her, and we head out toward the barn. Dad has about ten horses that are just for family. He and Mom ride every morning, and I want to take her to one of my favorite spots. However, there's not a chance in hell I am going to put her on a horse.

So, I asked Uncle Wyatt to do me a solid.

"Your farm is amazing," Hadley says as we go through the stable. "I've never seen anything like this."

"Dad rebuilt a lot after Granddad died. He wanted his legacy to really live on."

"He's done a remarkable job. Everything is beautiful, but still a horse farm, if you know what I mean?"

I laugh. "That's Mom's doing. She wanted everything to still look affordable. We sell not only racehorses, but to everyday farmers as well. Dad never wanted us to forget our roots, which is deep in Tennessee with farming. My mom's parents were one of the Hennington's first customers."

Sometimes it's easy to forget where you come from. While I have my other father's family, they've never really been like the Henningtons to me. They barely speak to Logan or I, the only time is to let us know how much we remind them of my dad. I can understand it, but when we moved here, we became MiMi and Grandad's blood, without sharing a drop of it.

Hadley wraps her hands around my arm and sighs. "I love all the history here. We both have that in common."

"It's probably why I didn't run out of your parents' house screaming."

"Daddy is intense, but you won him over."

She looks up at me and my chest tightens.

"What?" she asks as she studies my face.

"I didn't know I could love someone this much."

Her face softens and her smile reaches her eyes. "You're going to make me cry."

"That's not very hard to do lately."

"True."

I keep going until we reach the back and she gasps, hands flying to her mouth. "Cayden!"

We have a genuine sleigh that has two large gray horses hitched to it. Manny, our foreman is holding the reins. He claps me on the back as I take them, petting each of the horse's necks. "Well, are you going to just stand there or get in and go for a ride?"

We spend an hour riding through Tennessee farmlands, over to a spot that my family rode to all the time. Thankfully, the snow on the ground allowed us passage, I was worried, but we made it.

She rests her head on my shoulder and drinks her hot chocolate as I hold her to me. "If I knew I just had to get knocked up to get all this, I would've done it on purpose."

I laugh and rub her arm. "I think we would've ended up right here no matter what."

"I think you're right."

"Hold on," I pretend like I'm reaching for something.

"What?"

"I need my phone, I have to record you saying that."

Hadley snorts and then nestles herself back against me. "When do you want to get married?"

I hadn't thought much past this. "I don't know, when do you want?"

"Do you think we could do it before the baby comes? I know it's soon, but…I really would like to have it somewhat in order."

"I'd marry you today, Hadley."

Her mouth finds mine and the cold air fades away as we create our own heat and I am eternally grateful I get to spend the rest of my life with her.

Epilogue

HADLEY

~Six Weeks Later~

"There's no place like home, there's no place like home," Bethanne says over and over in my face as our families rush around the house, yelling at each other.

Yesterday, the Henningtons arrived in Sugarloaf and the calm, sweet mother I have known my whole life has become a crazy lady. She's insistent that everything be perfect, which is hilarious since nothing is perfect in our lives.

"Why is she like this?"

Beth shrugs. "You're her first kid and you're getting married in two hours. I'm surprised her head hasn't actually imploded by this point."

Great. "How is Daddy behaving?"

She grins. "Well, he took Cayden and Logan to the treehouse and I haven't seen them return. Cayden and Logan that is."

My eyes widen and fear grips me. I grab my sister's arms. "Find them."

"Please, he likes your fiancé...ohh, that's probably the last time we'll use those words. You're going to have a husband."

Lord save me from annoying sisters. "Get Mel and find the boys."

She gives me a salute and runs out.

I stare at myself in the mirror, heart racing as I see this woman there, all dressed in white and tears in her eyes. I can't believe I'm getting married today.

Cayden and I agreed to allow our parents the chance to throw us a proper wedding after both our mothers begged. I couldn't have cared less if we went to the courthouse, I actually thought it would've been kind of perfect since we're both lawyers, but Presley almost had a heart attack.

The bedroom door opens and Melanie enters. Her thick red hair is pulled back with curls hanging around her. "Hi, love."

"Hi."

"You are stunning."

"Thank you."

"I came up because your mother is fixing Bethanne's dress and I thought maybe you could use a drink, but you're pregnant, and can't, so I drank it for you. You're welcome."

"You need a therapist," I say with a laugh.

"Know a good one?"

"Yeah, actually, yo *mama!*"

We both laugh because Aunt Brenna is actually a therapist, so the joke is funny because it's true.

Mel stands next to me, looking at my reflection as well. "Actually, I'm here to give you this."

She hands me a letter and I recognize the handwriting immediately. "He wrote me a letter?"

"I have no idea. I didn't read it."

I snort. "There's a first. You went through my mail all the time."

My finger slides under the seal and I pull out the note.

Dear Hadley,

When we decided not to write our vows, a part of me was upset about that, more because I wanted to tell you in my own words what I vow to you. Of course, I promise all the things they make you say, but I want to give you even more. If I could, I'd give you the world, but I can't do that, so I give you my heart, my soul, my love and my promise that I will spend every day of my life trying to make you happy. I will protect you and our son with everything that I am.

We will fight, but I think we do that best, and know that even if we're on opposite teams, I'm always on your side. I will love you no matter how many times you lose to me.

I could say so much more, but I promised your mom and mine that I wouldn't make you cry. I love you. I can't wait for you to be my wife. I'll be waiting for you—always.

Yours,
Cayden

"Well, that was just unfair," I say, sniffing back the tears.

"No! You can't cry. I'll kill him."

"It was sweet."

Melanie dabs at my eyes and then fans them. "I'm sure it was, but you need to get to the barn without tears."

I grip her wrists, wanting to say all the things in my heart. She has no idea how much I adore her. "Mel…"

"No. Let me say this to you. I know I moved out and we don't get to have rice pudding for dinner or pizza daily anymore, but I want you to know that you are my best friend. I am so happy you found Cayden and banged him when I left that night."

I smile, knowing those words were about as close to an 'I love you' as I'll ever get.

"I'm glad I got drunk and pregnant too. It's nice to be a walking cliché."

"At least we both wear that badge of honor. I slept with my boss and now he's considering firing me."

I start to say something but before I can, Bethanne comes barreling through the door, slams it, and rests her back against it. "Hide me."

Mel rolls her eyes. "Seriously, you ripped the dress, let your mother fix it."

"That's not why, *Melanie*," she sneers her name. "You are never going to believe who they invited."

"Who?" I ask.

"Asher. Whitlock."

"You still have a thing for him?" I ask, not understanding the appeal. Sure, Sheriff Whitlock is freaking hot. We all know it, but my sister is obsessed with the man. She gets all tongue-tied and stupid each time he comes around.

"Of course. Have you seen his ass in uniform?" Bethanne sighs. "It's even nice in a suit. I bet his ass is perfect bare."

Melanie peeks out the window behind her and whistles. "Jesus, he got hotter. Who is that girl with him?"

Bethanne pushes Melanie aside. "That's the nanny, who is also Chief Bettencourt's daughter, Phoebe."

"Are you sure she's just the nanny? Look at the way he's looking at her."

My sister grunts. "Yeah, he's thinking: Hey, where did Olivia go, you're supposed to be watching her. You're fired and where is that gorgeous Arrowood girl? I want a dance with her."

"Fat chance, you're jailbait."

Beth huffs. "I'm twenty and Phoebe is only four years older than me. She was a senior when I was a freshman. Also, she's totally off limits."

"Which makes the sex hot," Mel says, egging Bethanne on.

I giggle at that because anything to piss my sister off is entertaining. However, we're on a time crunch here and this could get ugly really quick. "Could you guys maybe, you know, help with the veil and all that?"

Both turn to me and move quickly. "Shit. Sorry, worst maid of honor ever," Beth says as she grabs it.

There's a soft knock on the door and Mel goes to see who it is. "Hey, Uncle Connor."

"Melanie, you look beautiful as always."

"Wait until you see Hadley."

She pushes the door open and my father walks in, his eyes widen and he clutches his chest. "Wow."

"Do I look pretty, Daddy?"

He shakes his head, "No, baby, you're way more than that."

I smile and he approaches, hands out in front of him. The familiar feel calms me. I know these hands, the ones that wiped my tears when I was sad, built the treehouse so I had a safe place to go anytime, and always were there in case I fell. He leans in, kissing my cheek.

"Is it time?" I ask.

"As much as it pains me to say, yes, it's time."

The room suddenly becomes very active as my cousin and sister gather different items and Daddy loops my arm in his. Each step I take pulls my heart in different directions. I'm so happy to be marrying Cayden, ready to be his wife and be a family, but I'm sad for the little girl who will be gone. My name will change, erasing the past just a little.

We reach the barn doors where our family and friends are waiting, my cousin Austin on one side of the huge door and Sebastian on the other. Austin winks at me and I smile. The three of us were closest in age and always managing to get in trouble together.

All of us are now grown and living the lives we had worked so hard for.

"Are you ready?" Daddy asks.

"Yes and no," I say, my voice breaking at the end.

"I feel the same, but I know he loves you. He looks at you the way I look at your mother, which is the only reason I can take this walk with you."

I nod, working so hard to hold back the tears. "I love him too."

"Then let's go and let me place your hand in his, but know that if you ever reach for me, Hadley Arrowood, I'll be right there."

Those damn tears fall at that, and I kiss my daddy's cheek. "You will never know how grateful I am that you're my father and that you found me in that tree."

"Oh, sweetheart, it's me who is grateful."

I laugh, because if not, I'll cry all my makeup off.

Austin coughs. "Umm, are you planning to run away or get married?"

Dad looks to me and I smile. "Married."

They open the doors and I walk towards my destiny—Cayden.

* * * *

Also from 1001 Dark Nights and Corinne Michaels, discover Evermore and Say You Won't Let Go.

Sign up for the 1001 Dark Nights Newsletter
and be entered to win a Tiffany Key necklace.

There's a contest every month!

Go to www.1001DarkNights.com to subscribe.

**As a bonus, all subscribers can download
FIVE FREE exclusive books!**

Discover 1001 Dark Nights Collection Ten

DRAGON LOVER by Donna Grant
A Dragon Kings Novella

KEEPING YOU by Aurora Rose Reynolds
An Until Him/Her Novella

HAPPILY EVER NEVER by Carrie Ann Ryan
A Montgomery Ink Legacy Novella

DESTINED FOR ME by Corinne Michaels
A Come Back for Me/Say You'll Stay Crossover

MADAM ALANA by Audrey Carlan
A Marriage Auction Novella

DIRTY FILTHY BILLIONAIRE by Laurelin Paige
A Dirty Universe Novella

HIDE AND SEEK by Laura Kaye
A Blasphemy Novella

TANGLED WITH YOU by J. Kenner
A Stark Security Novella

TEMPTED by Lexi Blake
A Masters and Mercenaries Novella

THE DANDELION DIARY by Devney Perry
A Maysen Jar Novella

CHERRY LANE by Kristen Proby
A Huckleberry Bay Novella

THE GRAVE ROBBER by Darynda Jones
A Charley Davidson Novella

CRY OF THE BANSHEE by Heather Graham
A Krewe of Hunters Novella

DARKEST NEED by Rachel Van Dyken
A Dark Ones Novella

CHRISTMAS IN CAPE MAY by Jennifer Probst
A Sunshine Sisters Novella

A VAMPIRE'S MATE by Rebecca Zanetti
A Dark Protectors/Rebels Novella

WHERE IT BEGINS by Helena Hunting
A Pucked Novella

Also from Blue Box Press

THE MARRIAGE AUCTION by Audrey Carlan
Season One, Volume One
Season One, Volume Two
Season One, Volume Three
Season One, Volume Four

THE JEWELER OF STOLEN DREAMS by M.J. Rose

SAPPHIRE STORM by Christopher Rice writing as C. Travis Rice
A Sapphire Cove Novel

ATLAS: THE STORY OF PA SALT by Lucinda Riley and Harry
Whittaker

LOVE ON THE BYLINE by Xio Axelrod
A Plays and Players Novel

A SOUL OF ASH AND BLOOD by Jennifer L. Armentrout
A Blood and Ash Novel

FIGHTING THE PULL by Kristen Ashley
A River Rain Novel

VISIONS OF FLESH AND BLOOD by Jennifer L. Armentrout and
Rayvn Salvador
A Blood and Ash/Flesh and Fire Compendium

A FIRE IN THE FLESH by Jennifer L. Armentrout
A Flesh and Fire Novel

Discover More Corinne Michaels

Evermore
A Salvation Series Novella

I was poised to become partner at my law firm even before I became secretly engaged to my boss. After being humiliated by him on my wedding day, I can't face working for him any longer. So I quit, waving my middle finger on my way out.

Now the only things I'm poised for are unemployment and loneliness.

When an opportunity with Cole Security arises, it seems like the perfect way to run, all the way to Virginia Beach. I wasn't expecting my childhood sweetheart to be there. I definitely wasn't prepared that when we saw each other again, Benjamin Pryce would be so grown-up. So gorgeous. So Navy SEAL-ish.

And still the same guy who broke my heart when I was fifteen--and could do it again.

They say if you're fooled once, shame on them. The second time, it's on you. The third time, it's going to be me that runs... unless he can convince me to stay forevermore.

* * * *

Say You Won't Let Go
A Return to Me/Masters and Mercenaries Novella

Emily Young had two goals in her life:
1. Make it big in country music.
2. Get the hell out of Bell Buckle.

She was doing it. She was on her way, until Cooper Townsend landed backstage at her show in Dallas.

This gorgeous, rugged, man of few words was one cowboy she couldn't afford to let distract her. But with his slow smile and rough hands, she just couldn't keep away.

With outside forces conspiring against them, Cooper hires the McKay-Taggart team to protect her. Emily refuses to let Cooper get hurt because of her. All she wants is to hold onto him, but she knows the right thing to do is to let go...

The Lexi Blake Crossover Collection features a new novel by Lexi Blake and five books by some of her favorite writers:

Lexi Blake - Close Cover
Larissa Ione - Her Guardian Angel
J. Kenner - Justify Me
Corinne Michaels - Say You Won't Let Go
Carly Phillips - His to Protect
Susan Stoker - Rescuing Sadie

Come Back for Me

The Arrowood Brothers Book 1
By Corinne Michaels
Now Available

One night, eight years ago, she gave me peace.

No names.

No promises.

Just two broken people, desperate to quiet their pain and grief.

In the morning, she was gone and had taken my solace with her. I left for the military that day, vowing never to return to this small town in Pennsylvania.

When my father dies, I'm forced to go home to bury him. At least I'll finally be rid of his farm, which is grown over and tangled with memories I've fought to forget.

And that's when I find her. She's even more beautiful than I remember and has the most adorable kid I've ever seen.

Years have passed, but my feelings are the same, and this time I refuse to let her go. They say you can't bury the past, and they're right. Because when long-ago secrets are exposed, rocking us both to the core, I have no choice but to watch her walk away again…

* * * *

The farm is a mess, that's all I keep saying to myself. It's a nightmare. He hadn't maintained a single thing other than the diary equipment, which he would've had to keep up and running if he wanted to make enough money to buy his liquor.

Still, the fact that he let the land go, is unbelievable. What could've been a ten million plus inheritance is worth half that at best. It's going to take a hell of a lot of work to get it close to what we'd want to sell it for.

I'm walking in the field out to the left of the creek, the place that I would come to hide. The first time my father drank himself into a rage, I was ten, and Declan took the beating, shielding all of us and telling us to run and hide.

I didn't fully understand what had happened, just that my brother, who I loved, was screaming for me to go.

So I did.

I ran. I ran so hard that I wasn't sure I'd ever stop. I ran until my lungs struggled to get air. I didn't stop until I was where I thought no one could ever find me because Declan had something in his eyes I had never seen—fear.

I'm standing here, on the edge of the creek, looking up at the platform I built in the tree where I spent so many days and nights hiding from the hell that was in my house.

What a fucking mess.

Being here is the last place I want to be, but there's nothing I have to hide from anymore. I'm no longer that scared little boy, and there are no more monsters hiding in the house. Yet, I can't help but feel the pit in my stomach.

The quiet is almost loud as I stand here listening to the creek that used to lull me to sleep. The farmland is beautiful. I can't help but see the lush greens and deep pink hue of the setting sun in the sky, illuminating the clouds and making them look like cotton candy.

I close my eyes, lifting my face to the sky, hearing the sound of my breathing.

And then a thump from above causes my senses to kick in.

I look around, trying to see what it was.

Then a sniffle.

"Hello?" I call out, turning to the tree and the platform high in its branches.

There's a scuffle, the sound of feet shuffling on the wood. Someone is up there. It has to be a kid because a grown adult wouldn't be hiding up on that platform. However, whoever it is doesn't answer.

"Hello? I know you're up there," I say a little softer because I'm trying to be less scary. "You don't have to be afraid."

Another bit of movement and then a cry that is clearly in pain.

I don't wait, I move up the tree, using the wood steps my brothers helped me build so I would always be able to come here.

"I'm coming up. Don't be scared," I instruct, not wanting whoever is up there to fall off the scrap of wood.

I make it to the platform and a little girl is huddled in the corner. Her eyes are wide and full of fear. She doesn't seem much older than I was the first time I headed up here, but I'm not really around kids much, so I have no clue how old she really is. I do know all about the apprehension and the tears running down her face. I used to wear a similar expression in this spot.

"I won't hurt you, are you okay? I heard you cry."

She nods quickly.

"Okay, are you hurt?"

A tear falls down her cheek and she nods again, clutching her arm.

"Is it your arm?" I ask, knowing that's what it is. When she still doesn't speak, I try to remember what it felt like to be hurt and alone, hiding in a tree. "I'm Connor, and I used to live here. This was my favorite place on this whole farm. What's your name?"

Her lip trembles, and she seems to wrestle with whether she can answer me. In the end, her green eyes watch me like a hawk as she clamps her lips tight, letting me know she has no intention of speaking to me.

I take another step up the ladder and lean on the platform. "It's okay, you don't have to tell me."

I'll stay up here for as long as it takes to get her down.

She sits up, her brown hair falling around her face, and she sniffs before pushing it back. "You're a stranger," the little girl says.

"I am. You're right not to talk to strangers. Would it help if I told you that I was also a sort of police officer in the navy?"

Her eyes narrow, assessing me. "Police officers have uniforms."

I grin, smart kid. "That's right. I wore one, but I'm not working now since I'm on the farm. Can you tell me how you hurt your arm?"

"I fell."

"How'd you climb up here?"

She shifts a bit. "I didn't want anyone to find me."

My gut tightens as a million answers as to why this little girl is hiding up here with her arm in pain instead of running home for help. I have to keep myself under control and remember not everyone has a shitty home life. It could be anything.

"Why not?"

She worries her bottom lip. "Daddy said I wasn't supposed to leave the house, and I didn't want him to be angry." Then she wipes her nose with her arm and another tear falls. "I came here so I could wait for Mommy to come home."

I give her a knowing nod. "Well, I'm sure your daddy is worried about you. We should get you back home and get your arm looked at."

"He's going to be so mad." Her lip quivers.

Poor thing is terrified. Of her father or because she broke the rules, I'm not sure. I don't know who she is or who her father is, but she can't stay up here injured and scared. She'll fall. "How about I don't tell him where I found you if he doesn't ask."

She eyes me curiously. "You mean lie?"

"No, I just think that friends keep secrets, and we're friends now, right?"

"I guess so."

"Well, friend, you know my name is Connor, but I still don't know yours."

Her lips purse. "I'm Hadley."

"It's nice to meet you, Hadley. Can I help you down since your arm is hurt?"

Hadley's head bobs quickly.

I instruct her how to get close, and then she wraps her arm around my neck, holding on tightly as I get us both down without jostling her too much. When we get to the ground, I set her on her feet and squat.

We're eye to eye, and there's something about the way she looks at me—as though I'm her savior—that makes my heart ache.

"Is your arm okay?"

"It hurts." Her voice is small and holds a quiet tremor of pain. She moves it across the front of her body, cradling it closely.

"Can I look at it?"

Hadley is a tiny thing. Although, I have no frame of reference on how old she is, if this is a normal height for a kid, or I'm an idiot.

"Okay."

I take a look and there's some bruising and it's swollen, but nothing glaringly obvious that she broke it.

"Well, it doesn't look terrible, but I think we need to get you home so they can make sure it's not broken. Where do you live?"

She points across the creek to where the Walcott farm is.

"Is your last name Walcott?"

"Yup."

I smile. It's good to know they didn't sell off their farm. The Walcott's were good people. My mother and Mrs. Walcott were close friends. When Mom died, Jeanie would bring us food and make sure we still had pie every now and then. I loved her and was sad when she passed. Tim died about a month after her, and my father would say it was from a broken heart. I wish my father loved my mother enough to go die alongside her, but I wasn't that lucky.

I had no idea if someone bought it or if the property was passed down to someone. They never had kids of their own, but it seems it's still in the family.

"I'll walk you home and make sure you don't get hurt again. Do you want to cut across or would you rather I drive you?"

I see her worry, but there's no way I'm letting this kid go off on her own when she's hurt.

"We can walk."

"All right." I stand, put my hand out, and smile when she takes it, knowing I earned a little of her trust.

We make our way to her house, neither of us saying much, but then I feel her start to tremble. I can remember all too well not wanting to go home because my parents were going to be mad at me. Too many times I had the wooden spoon to my hide because my mother said to be back before dark and I'd wandered off, lost in the vast lands that looked the same, and one of my brothers had to come find me.

"How long have you lived here?" I ask, wanting to take her attention off her impending punishment.

"I grew up here."

"Yeah, and how old are you?"

"I'm seven."

She must've moved in right after I left. "You live here with your parents?"

"My daddy runs the farm with my mommy. She's also a teacher."

"They sound like nice folks."

Hadley looks away, and that feeling niggles at me again. I've lived my entire life based on trusting my instincts. In the military, it's kill or be killed. I had to rely on myself to know when something was a threat or not. Something about her demeanor has red flags going up all over.

"My parents probably aren't home, so you won't meet them."

I nod as though I don't see through what she's doing. I grew up making excuses as to all the reasons my friends couldn't come or my teachers shouldn't call. My father was sleeping, he wasn't home, he was on the tractor, or he was out of town. Anything I could say to deter someone from seeing anything. From finding a reason to ask questions.

Hiding wasn't just for me, it was for everything about me.

"Well, if they're not, I'll at least know you got home safely."

"Do you think I can come over sometime to climb your tree? It has steps and mine doesn't."

I grin at her. "Anytime, kid. My tree is your tree. And if you come by in the next few days, I can show you two other hiding spots my brothers and I built."

"Really? Cool!" Hadley lights up.

"Really."

We get toward the drive and there's someone at the car. Her dark brown hair falls down her back in waves and she's lifting a paper bag from her trunk. When she turns, our eyes meet, and my heart stops.

Her lips part as the groceries tumble to the ground forgotten as I come face to face with the woman who has haunted my dreams.

My angel has returned, only she isn't mine.

About Corinne Michaels

Corinne Michaels is a New York Times, USA Today, and Wall Street Journal bestselling author of romance novels. Her stories are chock full of emotion, humor, and unrelenting love, and she enjoys putting her characters through intense heartbreak before finding a way to heal them through their struggles.

Corinne is a former Navy wife and happily married to the man of her dreams. She began her writing career after spending months away from her husband while he was deployed—reading and writing were her escapes from the loneliness. Corinne now lives in Virginia with her husband and is the emotional, witty, sarcastic, and fun-loving mom of two beautiful children.

Discover 1001 Dark Nights

Paige ~ CLOSER by Kylie Scott ~ SOMETHING JUST LIKE THIS by Jennifer Probst ~ BLOOD NIGHT by Heather Graham ~ TWIST OF FATE by Jill Shalvis ~ MORE THAN PLEASURE YOU by Shayla Black ~ WONDER WITH ME by Kristen Proby ~ THE DARKEST ASSASSIN by Gena Showalter

COLLECTION SEVEN
THE BISHOP by Skye Warren ~ TAKEN WITH YOU by Carrie Ann Ryan ~ DRAGON LOST by Donna Grant ~ SEXY LOVE by Carly Phillips ~ PROVOKE by Rachel Van Dyken ~ RAFE by Sawyer Bennett ~ THE NAUGHTY PRINCESS by Claire Contreras ~ THE GRAVEYARD SHIFT by Darynda Jones ~ CHARMED by Lexi Blake ~ SACRIFICE OF DARKNESS by Alexandra Ivy ~ THE QUEEN by Jen Armentrout ~ BEGIN AGAIN by Jennifer Probst ~ VIXEN by Rebecca Zanetti ~ SLASH by Laurelin Paige ~ THE DEAD HEAT OF SUMMER by Heather Graham ~ WILD FIRE by Kristen Ashley ~ MORE THAN PROTECT YOU by Shayla Black ~ LOVE SONG by Kylie Scott ~ CHERISH ME by J. Kenner ~ SHINE WITH ME by Kristen Proby

COLLECTION EIGHT
DRAGON REVEALED by Donna Grant ~ CAPTURED IN INK by Carrie Ann Ryan ~ SECURING JANE by Susan Stoker ~ WILD WIND by Kristen Ashley ~ DARE TO TEASE by Carly Phillips ~ VAMPIRE by Rebecca Zanetti ~ MAFIA KING by Rachel Van Dyken ~ THE GRAVEDIGGER'S SON by Darynda Jones ~ FINALE by Skye Warren ~ MEMORIES OF YOU by J. Kenner ~ SLAYED BY DARKNESS by Alexandra Ivy ~ TREASURED by Lexi Blake ~ THE DAREDEVIL by Dylan Allen ~ BOND OF DESTINY by Larissa Ione ~ MORE THAN POSSESS YOU by Shayla Black ~ HAUNTED HOUSE by Heather Graham ~ MAN FOR ME by Laurelin Paige ~ THE RHYTHM METHOD by Kylie Scott ~ JONAH BENNETT by Tijan ~ CHANGE WITH ME by Kristen Proby ~ THE DARKEST DESTINY by Gena Showalter

COLLECTION NINE
DRAGON UNBOUND by Donna Grant ~ NOTHING BUT INK by Carrie Ann Ryan ~ THE MASTERMIND by Dylan Allen ~ JUST ONE WISH by Carly Phillips ~ BEHIND CLOSED DOORS by Skye Warren ~ GOSSAMER IN THE DARKNESS by Kristen Ashley ~ THE

CLOSE-UP by Kennedy Ryan ~ DELIGHTED by Lexi Blake ~ THE GRAVESIDE BAR AND GRILL by Darynda Jones ~ THE ANTI-FAN AND THE IDOL by Rachel Van Dyken ~ CHARMED BY YOU by J. Kenner ~ DESCEND TO DARKNESS by Heather Graham~ BOND OF PASSION by Larissa Ione ~ JUST WHAT I NEEDED by Kylie Scott

On Behalf of 1001 Dark Nights,

Liz Berry, M.J. Rose, and Jillian Stein would like to thank ~

Steve Berry
Doug Scofield
Benjamin Stein
Kim Guidroz
Tanaka Kangara
Asha Hossain
Chris Graham
Chelle Olson
Kasi Alexander
Jessica Saunders
Stacey Tardif
Dylan Stockton
Kate Boggs
Richard Blake
and Simon Lipskar

Printed in Great Britain
by Amazon

21106109R00068